Joolz Denby is an award-wi[...]st and illustrator. Her novel 'St[...]r New Crime Writer Of The [...]r shortlisted for The Orange [...]s Arts festivals, contemporary n[...], and literary conventions. When not travelling, she lives in Bradford in a house stuffed with cats, musicians, and curios. She is a sporadic gardener, a practising tattooist, and an obsessive reader who never quite manages to get enough sleep. This novella is the first of the 'Miss Larkin' series.

by Joolz Denby

novels
Stone Baby
Corazon
Billie Morgan
Borrowed Light

poetry
Mad, Bad & Dangerous To Know
Emotional Terrorism
The Pride of Lions
Errors of the Spirit
Pray For Us Sinners

A True Account Of The Curious Mystery Of Miss Lydia Larkin And The Widow Marvell.

The Enigma Revealed.

or

What Really Happened In The Fateful Garden.

Joolz Denby

Published by Ignite Books

ISBN: 978-0-9567786-0-4

Typeset by Steve at Ignite.

Printed and bound by
Bell & Bain Ltd
Glasgow.

Dedication

Dedicated to the memory of my father, Captain Ron Mumford - a soldier, scholar of history both actual and mythological, and a gentleman.

Acknowledgements

My sincere thanks go to Steve Pottinger without whose dedication, belief and sheer hard work this book would never have seen the light of day; to my dear friend and Athene personified, Dr. Christine Alvin; to Mik Davis for his unflagging desire to stick it to the Man and his encouragement to me to do likewise; and to Justin Sullivan for his many, many years of unfailing support and kindness.

My thanks and respect also to the Goddess, as always.

Prologue

In modern times all is explained, from the humblest earthly microbes to the farthest starry reaches of the mighty Universe. Examined and then either accepted, or rejected and banished, by the cold, dissecting blades of Science. Retired and now un-worshipped gods and demons live on only in the pages of crumbling old books mouldering in neglected libraries, side by side with faeries, elves, spooks, barguests, Chatterchains, The Gentry, Wise Women, Men Of The Woods and the rustic Arts. White Magic, Green Magic and the laying on of hands, all filed under fantasy, all smiled at indulgently or derided as the quaint cobwebbed tatters of a bygone age. Sometimes they are resurrected by the television or films when the fashion for such relics of witchery and the Dark prevails, but only in the most superficial way, diluted to special effects by the anodyne power of Hollywood.

So in general, the Mystic Arts remain the twilight province of silly young Goths in cheap crushed velvet costumes and big shoes, or patently ridiculous older women in quasi-robes and stiffly hennaed hair selling 'magical' trinkets in tiny, incense-smelling over-priced New Age boutiques. The Weird or Alchemical, the Far-Seeing or the Mysterious and Glamoured could not possibly have power, or even any actuality, in the clean controllable modern world - the urban world, the world of instantaneous mass communications, the all-seeing eye of the Internet and that rigidly inescapable cultural regulator, television.

And certainly none of the aforementioned foolish, superstitious, mis-guided things are possible in a perfectly normal garden in a rather unfashionable part of town.

Are they?

1

Chapter One

Miss Larkin - she actually preferred 'Ms.' as she was a divorcée and so no longer a Mrs. or a Miss, but no-one seemed to use the useful title Ms. anymore - had bought Number 26, Croyd Terrace some six months ago, having searched for it, or rather the place the undistinguished narrow house at the end of a cul-de-sac shielded on two sides by a tall factory wall, stood on, for many years. That it was so cheap as to be almost unseemly was due to a war that raged unchecked between Number 26's owners and the family in Number 24. The Glydes could not wait to get as far away as possible from the vulgar Oulthwaites, and the Oulthwaites could not disguise their loathing of the snobbish Glydes. Such at any rate were their opinions of each other.

It was a classic Neighbour War, described in unfortunate detail by Sara Glyde over shortbread and Earl Grey when Miss Larkin arrived for her appointment to view. During Mrs. Glyde's tense monologue the distorted racket of Bill Haley's 'Rock Around The Clock' vibrated through the wall from next door at full volume. This barrage of archaic music was apparently a device hit upon by the Oulthwaites to put off potential buyers and thus further annoy the Glydes, though why the Oulthwaites should wish to do this was a puzzle to Miss Larkin: surely they would want to encourage buyers and thus more swiftly rid themselves of the Glydes? But apparently things had got to such a pass that revenge, however misguided and counter-productive, was the only desirable goal.

Conflict had escalated after the Glydes, naturally enough it seemed to them, had complained about the dreadfulness of Mrs. Oulthwaite's passionate love for outdoor fairy lights and garden statuary of the Cheeky Frog variety. Not just at Christmas, mind you, Mrs. Glyde had hissed at Miss Larkin, her little finger crooked white and rigid on the handle of her bone-china Zodiac mug (Virgo), while Mr. Haley crooned about rockin' till broad daylight, those lights were up *all year round*. And the figurines - just awful.

'Ah.' Miss Larkin had murmured neutrally.

Mrs. Glyde had bridled fiercely. 'And the lights are all over the garden - in the bushes, the tree, her dreadful Pound Shop pergola, you name it. All different colours. Flashing. I can't tell you how distressing it is. Of course the children - the ones from The Terrace, not my children, they're grown up now, Lucy is at University in Wales - well, those children think it's wonderful, they do nothing but hang around making nuisances of themselves. It's like Blackpool Illuminations - so dreadful - so - so . . . *Common*.'

'Hmm,' Miss Larkin had remarked and then stirred her weak tea unnecessarily. She had eaten the shortbread quite quickly, partly out of nerves and partly because she loved shortbread, even bought shortbread. She was nervous because she wanted the house for various private reasons. She wanted it very badly indeed, if the truth be told, and not because of the B&Q mod cons or carefully neutral colour scheme as dictated by television décor gurus. She would not have cared if the Glydes had painted it day-glo purple glitter throughout. That kind of detail was immaterial and could easily be fixed. No, in this case it really was location, location, location.

Mrs. Glyde had seemed about to embark on another tirade when the kitchen door had banged open, setting the mugs on the mug-tree shivering and a lanky, six-foot youth in baggy jeans sitting just under his bony bottom and revealing his undies to the world had stumped in. Weighed down by swags of heavy key chains the jeans seemed in imminent danger of giving in to gravity and the youth in some peril of being overwhelmed by a monstrous jut of eye-concealing straightened fringe and the inordinate quantity of spots embroidering

4

his sallow cheeks with inflamed knots. *Poor little thing*, thought Miss Larkin, *how hard it is to be young, such a burden.*

The youth had stormed past his mother - the Glyde nose being in strong possession of both the faces viewed by Miss Larkin - and opening the huge fridge had fiercely chugged Coca-Cola straight from a litre bottle.

'William! Please! How many times have I….' Mrs. Glyde had bridled furiously.

The youth had turned his oystery gaze upon his mother. 'Off out,' he'd muttered as if moving his lips fully would result in terrible consequences. His mother had begun to speak, then shut her mouth as William sauntered out slamming the front door behind him. Tears had glazed Mrs. Glyde's eyes. Miss Larkin was not surprised. It was obvious to her that William's mother loved him more than anything in the world and failed to see that beneath the thin, friable veneer of youthful rebellion, William loved her just as much. Such, had pondered Miss Larkin as she often did, is the great problem of families. Lack of faith. Lack, indeed, of communication. In her lap, concealed by the yellow pine table, her long, slim fingers glittering with subtle rings worth more than the entire contents of Mrs. Glyde's house, if not the house itself, had moved in a short complex pattern. The air around them had seemed, if you were the noticing type, which Mrs. Glyde wasn't, to shimmer slightly with a pale glittering mauve iridescence. A faint scent of sandalwood briefly floated through the room. Doubtless Mrs. Glyde thought it was her plug-in air freshener.

Sara Glyde had looked slightly discombobulated. Her pink frosted lips had opened in a complaining rictus but then she seemed to pause, as if her mind was stuttering. 'I - er... That boy - really.... I - he's - oh. I love him so much, do you see how handsome he is? Such lovely thick hair just like his father's before he receded and he's grown so tall and - and he's so clever, so intelligent, you should see him on his computer, so technical, I - I - oh.'

Miss Larkin had known that was not what Mrs. Glyde had intended to say, but that Mrs. Glyde felt strangely happy and liberated for saying it.

'Yes,' said Miss Larkin, 'he seems a *very* nice boy.'

The house sale went through without a hitch, despite the best efforts of the Oulthwaites' rock and roll onslaught, and the Glydes had professed themselves very glad to get away from an area that was, in their opinion, going rapidly downhill. They kindly wished Miss Larkin the best of British when she had to deal with the Oulthwaites. The Glydes firmly believed they had been very, very clever in the way they had dealt with Miss Larkin and patted themselves on the back for having achieved their asking price so easily and therefore making a tidy profit on a house they had inherited from Mr. Glyde's mother at no cost to themselves (other than the outlay for copious amounts of neutral-coloured paint). They thought they had successfully persuaded the obviously unworldly Miss Larkin to part with far more cash than the property was worth, little knowing the unworldly purchaser of their property was in a position to pay a thousand times the asking price and considered she had a bargain. She wanted the house for reasons they could never have comprehended. But the Glydes were thrilled. This windfall enabled them to buy up into a much nicer area. In the years that followed, when people spoke of the Glydes, they always said it was completely charming, the way Mrs. Glyde so obviously adored her son Will, and that the youth was, despite the clothes and the hair, a very *nice* boy.

Miss Larkin was most satisfied and moved herself and her inordinately large black cat, Dion, in straight away.

She rather liked the fairy lights, though she never quite reconciled herself to the Cheeky Frog. Neither did Dion.

Chapter Two

'They did what?' queried Hester Marvell, or The Widow Marvell as she preferred, as Lydia poured more Darjeeling, aromatic with an added cardamom pod and a clove, into her old china cup. The fragrant steam coiled upwards sinuously like some glorious, ephemeral incense. Today's cake, baked earlier by Lydia, had been a yoghurt sponge soaked in rose and lemon syrup, scattered with preserved rose petals and a sprinkle of edible silver glitter. Lydia served it on mismatched antique porcelain with equally mismatched old silver cutlery and Turkish rose jam. Hester proclaimed it unnecessarily decadent - *Why do your cakes sparkle, Lyddie? It's most singular* - but had none the less managed to consume two generous portions. She found she had quite an appetite these days, unusual for an abstemious person such as herself, but the rigours of house-moving and the excitement that had attended on her purchasing the house next door to Lydia so soon after they had met - or as she couldn't help feeling, *re*-met - had revived her animal spirits, or as much as she had. Now she was settling nicely into her new abode, and the loneliness she had suffered for so long was lifted. Life was good, she thought, and it's not a crime to be happy. In moderation, of course. She allowed herself a slight smile.

Lydia smiled back with a good deal more vigour, and her voice contained a definite giggle. 'They played rock and roll music very loudly every time the Glydes had a buyer round - really. I seem to remember it was Bill Haley the day I viewed. 'Rock Around The Clock'. I'm not sure what it was meant to achieve other than to thoroughly irritate the Glydes. They hated each other so much that logic, as my old teacher used to say, had quite flown out of the window. Dion, stop that! Greedy boy.'

Hester made a noise that could only be described as harrumphing, were such a restrained and tastefully attired figure, slim to the point of emaciation and with a perpendicular air, indeed capable of harrumphing. Dion gazed at her tolerantly with his huge topaz eyes then returned to trying to steal jam, an occupation he excelled in. 'So it would seem. Well, I'm much happier now I've finally finished the decorating, or to be truthful, Mr. Baggott has finished the decorating. The Oulthwaites left behind eight different patterns of wallpaper and as for the bathroom - dolphins. Mother and baby dolphins blowing bubbles.'

'Now you sound like Sara Glyde. Have you done it all in beige?'

'Cream, if you don't mind, Madam. With hints of Ming Blue. The bathroom anyway. The living room has a tinge of ochre.'

'Ming Blue? How lovely. Like your dress - is it new?'

'To me, yes. The finest Marie Curie could offer. It's a Monsoon. I got a slub linen cardi to match as well. The young vendeuse was of the opinion no one would have bought either piece as they were - what did she say? *Well dull.* Her eye was on the fuchsia sequin strapless circa 1983, I believe. It was *proper retro.* Or so she said.'

Hester sniffed and looked down at her tea cup modestly. The keen observer might have noticed a faint smile on her pale lips. She was doing a lot of smiling these days, it was really quite exhilarating.

Lydia smiled too, amused as ever by Hester's turn of phrase and pleased to look at her friend's appearance which made her think of a kind of secular nun dressed by Balmain in 1935, and tucked a stray lock of artfully fair hair that had escaped from her twist back behind an ear decorated with rather large, platinum and diamond set opal teardrop earrings, or as she persisted in calling them, 'earbobs'. As Lydia was otherwise dressed in her usual Winter uniform of loose fitting old jeans, a faded, mis-shapen bobbly rose-pink cashmere sloppy-joe sweater and tan sheepskin boots, the effect of the earrings was charmingly bohemian. Her figure was, as they say in the

8

magazines, curvy, so she looked immensely cuddly. This type of ensemble fitted her persona of an artist, of the sort who did portraits by commission and illustrations for magazines and books, rather well. Naturally, real artists of that type were generally unable to afford earrings of that calibre, but so well did Lydia mimic this stereotype that no-one - except Hester who observed and noted everything - seemed to notice the jewels, thinking rather that Miss Larkin always looked so nice, smelled so lovely and had such pretty things. This persona - so unthreatening, so feminine - enabled Lydia quietly to go to places and visit with people most would think scary, if not downright dangerous. But Lydia was never frightened of any-one, and certainly not of the living.

She smiled again at Hester, reminding herself to find something very nice for her forthcoming birthday. 'Well done, that woman. Excellent bargain. You look like a painting by a later Pre-Raphaelite - rather silvery-watery, in a good way - perhaps a Nixie or some kind of nymph.'

Hester snorted. 'Nymph? Hardly. Not at my advanced age. I shall be in possession of my bus pass next year. I wonder what becomes of elderly nymphs, or indeed anything along those lines? Would they retire, do you think? Or go to the Old Nature Spirits Home? One could only speculate what such an establishment might be like. Rather fun, I would think. I wonder if there's a retired gods' home, too? A much more soignée establishment of course, I should think, very toney. I wonder if they'd take non-deities? It'd beat The Pines Rest Home For Gentlewomen In Reduced Circumstances and no mistake.'

Lydia coughed and took a sip of tea, her cheeks pink. 'Excuse me - the remnants of that Yuletide flu. I expect they just - well, just fade away. Or something. You know. More cake?'

'No, thank you Lyddie. I really must watch my waistline - and that cat has eaten all the jam again.' Dion gave Hester what is some-times called an old fashioned look and strolled to his cat bed - or as

Hester called it, his chaise-longue - and attended to his toilet. Black against black fleece, he was invisible except for twin seams of fiery gold which showed he was not quite yet asleep: sleeping, Hester avowed, was Dion's profession. Lydia agreed, but she knew why Dion slept and slept - he'd had a very hard life.

Lydia busied herself clearing the table, sweeping crumbs into her hand and dropping them into a chipped Willow Pattern bowl for the birds that Dion was too lazy to hunt. While Hester browsed an early bulb catalogue Lydia loaded the dishwasher and then rinsed her soft hands under the tap, admiring the sparkle of her diamonds and the intense blue of her big sapphire. Outside a silver-gilt winter sun slanted low across the yard at the side of the house where her black Chrysler 'gangster car' as Hester called it, was parked next to a chaotic array of large pots containing ailing plants and trees Lydia had rescued for pennies from the nearby B&Q garden centre. Wiping her hands on a tea towel, Lydia sighed. The black bamboo wasn't happy, really, the way it had been let to dry out, it was.... She was fully aware she was deliberately not thinking about certain things but forgave herself as you couldn't think about everything at once. Or at least, she couldn't, though she had known people who could. Not that it made them happy, she sighed, far from it. Then another thought struck her, rather forcibly.

'Hester - are you - please forgive me for prying - actually in reduced circumstances?'

Hester replaced her teacup on its non-matching saucer. 'Not yet, Lyddie. Not yet. I was left provided for to some extent. Mr. Marvell, being considerably older than myself as you know, was very keen to ensure I was looked after. He was good like that. But not a millionaire. His experiments took up a lot of our income, though as you know, we did have some success which brought us a tidy sum. If I live an unconscionably long time I will find myself facing The Pines. Really, it doesn't pay to expect that telegram from Her Majesty these days. Not unless you enjoy being fed gruel by some chit of a girl in a room full of your drooling peers. I would rather not, thank you. I am hoping for a convenient pneumonia, personally, when I reach my dotage.'

'Hester! Please, you really need not worry about things like that. You know - how I'm placed, you'll never go anywhere so horrible, I promise you. I have more than enough for us both, for as long as we need.'

Hester looked at Lydia thoughtfully. By the radiator Dion stirred and stretched, shivering his fur into ebony ripples. 'I know you have, Lyddie, and I'm grateful, very grateful that you should think of me. I know how kind you are. Just getting the house has made me feel so much - better. Yes, better. Safer, if you like. I can't thank you enough for suggesting it.'

Lydia sighed, and reaching out patted Hester's hand, feeling the narrow, articulated bones beneath the soft, pale skin etched with tiny splatters of acid burns and faint discolorations from the chemicals and substances used in Mr. Marvell's experiments. Hester's hand was warm, human, life pulsing in the bluish veins.

'Well, the likes of us should stick together, shouldn't we?' she said.

Chapter Three

Lydia had met Hester six years ago. It had been a cool, Autumn day with the scent of fallen leaves and the heathery-peaty dust of the nearby moor lands permeating even the higgledy-piggledy town centre. At that point Lydia was living in a village about ten miles away, and had been in the Big City - as she ironically called it - buying books and new underwear, when passing through the square she noticed a stall promoting Amnesty International, a cause she rather favoured. There was a petition to release some Tibetan activists - Lydia was very fond of Tibet - and she bent to sign it. Straightening up she saw a thin woman, draped in varying shades of sage green and eyeing her coolly from still, grey eyes under straight dark brows.

'Thank you for signing. Would you care for a leaflet, or even a badge? Excellent Glamour, by the way, most convincing, I really must congratulate you.' The woman's voice was very even, but quivered faintly with suppressed excitement. Her almond-shaped face appeared completely calm.

Lydia was so surprised she dropped the biro. Flustered, she stooped to pick it up and again straightened up to look at what she now realised was a very remarkable woman indeed. The first person, in fact, who had ever seen through her little veil.

'Why, thank you.' Lydia knew there was no use pretending she didn't know what the woman was talking about. That was obvious. 'If you don't mind my saying, you're not an adept. So how do you...?'

Small boys on skateboards skirled past in the chill breeze, shouting incoherently. The distant sound of traffic and the mechanical trilling of a mobile phone seemed to recede to silence. The damp, greenish shadow of the ornate clock tower lengthened over the square and a faint unlikely scent of vetiver and salt caused a passing pensioner to blink as a long buried memory surfaced, then sank like a trout breaching in a dark pond.

The woman allowed herself a small smile, Mona Lisa fashion. 'My late husband, Mr. Marvell, was a *Gentleman*. I am his relict, Hester Marvell.'

The word, Gentleman, was uttered with a particular modulation and a certain slight movement of the left hand that explained all to Lydia. Lilies replaced vetiver and the air appeared to shimmer slightly. Then it stilled.

Hester continued. 'He was one of the most - well, I daresay modesty is of no use in this case, he was the leading Magus of the North. Such a lovely man and so kind. He was a great deal older than myself. He died over ten years ago now. I am myself a mere student, struggling to comprehend his legacy.' She made a slight, rather archaic bow, which Lydia acknowledged.

'I think we should have a coffee,' Lydia said firmly. 'Can you leave all this to that young man scurrying towards us with such purpose on his face? There's a Starbucks over there.'

'Toby? Oh yes of course, a tireless worker. Toby! I've met an old chum, so if you don't mind, I'll take my break now - yes, thank you, lovely to catch up, indeed.'

Ensconced in the coffee house, with an espresso for Hester and a hot chocolate for Lydia (with cream & chocolate sauce) they gazed at each other in silence, then smiled like conspiratorial schoolgirls.

Hester made another small gesture and the faint green scent of white roses mingled briefly with the odours of cake, damp people and hot coffee. The two women now seemed to the other customers of Starbucks to be merely a pair of gossiping middle-aged women, of no possible interest to anyone. 'I hope you don't mind, I thought we might need privacy.'

'No, good idea - and nicely done, too. I see you use the Gramercy

13

System. So useful.' Lydia drank some chocolate through a straw to avoid a cream moustache.

'Indeed. My late husband was a considerable exponent of the style. I am only, as I say, a student of such things.' Hester shrugged diffidently, but not without satisfaction at her ability.

'Oh, more than a simple student - Mrs. Marvell...'

'Hester, please. And you...?'

Lydia thought for a second then decided on caution. 'Lydia. Lydia Larkin. Miss. Or rather, Ms. - but no one seems to use that anymore, do they? I am - divorced. A long time ago - a very long time ago.'

Hester thought for a moment. 'I won't ask how long. Time is of course, merely a mode of thought. I assume - and please correct me if I'm wrong - that you are an adept of some standing? In the Western Tradition? I know you are projecting a Glamour that has almost permanent qualities and it's marvellously done, if I may say so, but beneath that I cannot penetrate - not, I hasten to add, that I would be so rude as to pry. But really, what are you doing *here?*' She gestured gracefully at the coffee-house and the shabby, provincial English town beyond its plate-glass windows.

Lydia took another creamy sip and smiled; as she did so the air seemed to gleam with a golden haze and a young couple nearby - she with spiky pink hair, soft features and many facial piercings, he a carbon copy of Will Glyde - suddenly stopped trying to be cool and gazed at each other with rapturous adoration.

'Oh, you know. You have to live somewhere. This seemed like a good enough place and as you know, the area has certain - qualities. I'm sure your late husband knew that. I got tired of travelling, always moving. I found - a very good house, in Ravensbury.'

Hester looked surprised. 'In Ravensbury? But it's - well. I'm surprised. Is it...?'

'Oh very, very well located. Directly above a four-way crossing, an axis, really. My living room is absolutely above the centre. The last occupant's mother lived there for over fifty years. She was a hundred and twenty when she died, though of course the family didn't realise that. Or anything else, thankfully. The whole structure, and the land around it, is permeated with essence. Quite extraordinary.'

Hester stirred her coffee. 'So that's where it is. We did wonder. We tapped into the emanations from our workroom, but never.... Ravensbury. Indeed. It just shows that one should clear one's mind of all prejudice, even the tiniest. I would never have thought that in a place like that.... Ah, well.'

Lydia reached forward and touched Hester's arm. 'I'm so sorry, I didn't mean to upset you....'

'Not at all, not at all. It's just a surprise. So close - and yet.... But at least you - someone responsible - have it now. I hate to think what would have happened if someone - unsuitable - had found it. I take it you'll be pursuing the craft? Are you working on anything currently? I would offer my services if I thought I could be of any use...?'

Lydia looked at Hester, seeing, as she always did, for good or ill, the truth behind the mask. It would have been a simple matter to discover everything that made up the complex, subtle creature that was Hester Marvell, but Lydia felt that would be rude. Many times, in her past, before she withdrew from such things, Lydia routinely scanned people she met, on the grounds of security. But she had tired of it. She had tired of seeing every flaw and false hope, every furtive sin, petty cruelty and disappointed dream, so apart from a brief glimpse to ensure her safety and privacy would not be affected, she tended to let well alone. Less is more, as her old mentor always said. Let's deal only with what we need to use, complexity for its own sake is an error beloved of the charlatan.

Lydia, using the simplest of arts, could see easily that Hester was a profoundly honest and scrupulous person. She had an over-developed sense of duty and the clear, precise mind of a scientist.

Within her shell of dry humour and self-deprecation, there burnt a restrained but passionate heart. Hester had loved her late husband devotedly, that was obvious, and she had respected him profoundly for his abilities, intelligence and what Lydia sensed was his great kindness. She mourned him honestly and unashamedly and felt comfortable with that, not bowing to modern conventions of 'effecting closure' and 'moving on'. Hester didn't want to move on, she wanted to savour her loving memories. She had resisted trying to contact Mr. Marvell, doubtless feeling it was vulgar and selfish to do so. Lydia approved of that sentiment. She saw there was a shadow in Hester's past, the faint, distant cry of a child in pain, and a presence buried even deeper in Hester's DNA that cast a curious influence on her persona, but Lydia did not pursue either thing. If Hester wished to confide in her, she would. If not, it would be unmannerly to spy on her.

A sudden breeze whipped across the square, and Lydia saw Toby talking animatedly to another young man in fashionably tight clothes. The wind stirred up dust-devils of crisp-packets and sweetie-wrappers, and a young woman clutched at her flared skirt in the age-old gesture of female modesty as the breeze lifted it. In the café, the young lovers held hands and kissed lingeringly, quickly drawing a stern look of disapproval and pursed-lipped tutting from an older, matronly woman nearby. Lydia wove a little pattern with her finger-tips and, again, the air glimmered for a second and the woman gasped, smelling the lilacs she had loved in her grandmother's garden in Scotland, remembering what it felt like to be young, remembering the gangling, brown-eyed youth who had escorted her to the village dance so carefully. She gathered up her bags and hurried out of the café.

Hester raised an eyebrow. 'Well, well, an act of charity. That was kind - to her husband. And her, of course. And - are you satisfied with what you see? Thank you for being so discreet, I hardly felt a thing.'

16

Lydia smiled, her cheeks pink at being caught out. 'Ah - well. As to the charity - one should always try to improve rather than reprove, don't you think? More coffee?'

'Interesting. Improve rather than reprove. You've read Master Gyremandel? I had thought Mr. Marvell had the last remaining copy of his Meditations. Such a thoroughly humane teacher, I always thought, so - what is that modern expression? Grounded. But generally unheard of these days, or indeed for the last six hundred years. Where did you come across him?'

Lydia didn't like lying. The necessity of falsehood was threaded through her life like a black stitch but it still irked her. She waved a glittering hand negligently. 'Oh, you know - scraps here and there, a fragment, this and that. I agree, a lovely philosophy. If you still have the book I'd love to read it.'

Gyremandel's brown, agile face suddenly flooded her mind; she saw again the little white temple overlooking the wine-dark sea, then the stormy reaches of the Eastern mountains lightning-etched against the tumultuous night sky as Gyremandel rode furiously through the driving rain trying to escape his Inquisitors. So sad. He had been such a brilliant mind. But this would never do. She must live in the present, not in dreams.

'It would be my pleasure to lend it to you. I feel I almost knew him sometimes, his voice in writing is so very clear. It's dedicated to your namesake, did you know? The Muse Lydia - in Latin of course. He had such beautiful Latin.'

'Really? How extraordinary, I feel positively honoured. I do think, Hester, that we should meet again. Would you be agreeable?'

Hester bowed her head, her shining cap of short dark-silver hair gleaming in the dull light from the window. Lydia thought she looked very clean, spare and polished and she liked that immensely.

'I can't think of anything I'd like more, Lydia. If I may be so bold, I feel as if I had known you for years. As Master Gyremandel said, we are all brethren borne along in the great river of Time.

Perhaps that should have been sisteren, too.'

'Autre temps, autre mores - he meant that, I'm sure.'

And they exchanged phone numbers.

That night Hester dreamt she was walking slowly along a vast, windswept beach beneath a luminously blue sky. The white sand blew across her path in rippled imitation of the sea. She felt calm and rather happy but in a formless way as she walked on and on. Eventually she spied coming towards her a dark figure. As the figure got closer she saw it was a woman. As the woman drew near, Hester realised it was actually the shape of a woman formed from a mass of living honey bees, and that the woman-shape was Lydia. The bee-hair danced and swirled in the breeze, the draperies of the bee-dress fluttered and the bee-lips smiled lovingly. The air was saturated with the scent of honey, clover and ozone; Hester knew all too well the hidden power of perfumes and her dream-self desperately tried to memorise the combination. The muted hum of the insects seemed to Hester to mimic human speech: *hello Hester, such a long time since last we met. Yes,* Hester replied, *isn't it.* And it seemed to her she knew why Lydia was made of bees and why they had known each other before, but strain as she might, the knowledge slipped from her grasp like the blown sand. *Never mind,* said the bees, said Lydia, *Time is but a mode of thought. We're together again in this Now and that's all that matters.* And the bee-Lydia dispersed into a mass of little insects that flew off into the distance leaving Hester alone on the beautiful beach.

The dream faded and Hester fell into a long, delicious, peaceful sleep.

In the morning she had honey, instead of marmalade, on her toast.

Chapter Four

Winter turned slowly into Spring and Lydia's wild, fecund garden began to burst with all kinds of blossoms and explode with greenery; leaves unfurling, tendrils coiling, the stand of six birch trees putting on their most lovely, tender jade veils. Sheltered in the crook of the factory's great brick walls that held and reflected heat, the garden, unusually large for the area, had an almost tropical microclimate that saw vegetation growing with a rich, lush velocity. Bees buzzed lazily amongst the haphazard mass of blossoms on the apple and cherry trees and the first early yellow roses falling in a cascade of sunshine down the garage wall. The chocolate smell of clematis 'Montana' drifted on the breeze from the tumbledown shed where it fought for climbing space with a huge blush pink 'Paul's Himalayan Musk' rose. An enormous white rose gloriously named 'The Rambling Rector' threatened to engulf the old rowan by the hedge with thousands of small, delicate white single flowers, and in the shade, native bluebells and primroses glimmered. The remnants of swathes of daffodils and crocuses faded in pastel tatters, and the lawn, an utter disgrace, brilliant green but heavily embroidered with daisies, grew unchecked until the ever-useful Mr. Baggot shoved and grunted around it with a lawnmower not much younger than himself.

Dion, his long, attenuated limbs stretched out to their fullest extent, took possession of an old wooden bench - once painted periwinkle blue but now much faded - that faced into the sun and lay dozing for hours, occasionally rousing himself to eat an early butterfly. Lydia reproved him for this habit and he lazily licked her hand, flirted with her briefly, but refused to give up his treats and eyed the small pond which would be shortly filled with tadpoles which he felt would be a fine dessert, if he could only catch them without wetting his beautiful, henna-black fur.

Hester's garden was altogether a more formal affair now the abandoned Cheeky Frog had found its way to the Oxfam shop along with its comrades, the assorted gnomes and resin fairies who had twirled their skirts and kissed their hands to no-one in particular. It was slowly being given up to a neat vegetable garden and a herb and antique Damask rose parterre bordered in box and containing rather more than the usual garden herbs, guarded by an old carved wooden owl. There was a large stone and brass sundial featuring a sailing-boat gnomon next to a shaded wooden swing seat, and Hester had left the remaining white solar lights, even adding some of her own. Tastefully, of course. Her garden would have pleased any gardener with its tidy grace and fertility, but in comparison to the burgeoning earth of Lydia's plot it was as blanched as the roots and leaves Hester used in her various strange decoctions, many of which ended up on the compost where they collapsed in puffs of violet, saffron, crimson or viridian smoke, filling the air with heady or dizzy-ing vapours - one memorably perfuming the entire Terrace for two days with the milky, caustic odour of green almonds tinged with mandrake. Hester was quite glad she had refrained from trying that one on anything living, including herself.

Hester's garden lights and the new, fascinatingly strange garden design (they were more used to battered concrete patios damp with mould, pocked with burnt out barbecues and haunted by deceased plastic furniture) delighted the children from The Terrace. They had been more than a little worried that 'The New Ladies' at the end of the cul-de-sac might be more Glyde-like than Oulthwaitian and the fairy garden that twinkled across the Backs like re-assuring beacons in the night might be turned off forever leaving them to the darkness of their childish dreams. The resurgence and elaboration of their shrine satisfied them mightily. Led by their chief, Joey Delaney, and assisted by his faithful lieutenants Rav and Tiff, the Terrace Crew watched with the desperate and unrelenting patience of ten year olds and the native cunning of the street urchin as The Ladies expanded in the warming Spring.

Lydia was naturally aware from the moment she moved in of the Crew's interest in both herself and Hester. She liked children and was prepared to be fully scrutinised and have their unclouded and impartial judgement passed upon herself and her friend, and could only hope that the judgement would be positive. She felt confident that she would pass muster, but with a child, you never knew. Dion was more of a problem in terms of his unpredictable relationships with humans of any age, but he could always be bribed into goodish behaviour with black olives, a rather un-feline food he adored.

That it was Autumn when she arrived had meant the children were largely confined to their homes by their families, and passed the idle hours with their Nintendos and the ever-present glowing eye of the television, a device that throned over their and their families' lives unchallenged. They seldom ventured out after school because their families were obsessed with child-murderers and other grotesques of the media age and were as frightened of the night as medieval peasants. Not for them the tender, moist shrouding of a star-set dark filled with the scents of damp earth and crushed foliage, blooming like a great black rose, velvety and secret; the night was a place you made your compacts with sin and the hiding place of wickedness. They would have been outraged to see Lydia and Hester, well wrapped up in the blankets crocheted by Hester over the years, sipping hot chocolate on the swing seat at gone two in the morning and discussing the phases of the moon best for planting hellebore.

But with Spring came the sound of piping voices and the ear-splitting screech of untended bicycle brakes. Soon the front yard, with its array of mis-matched, mossy old terracotta pots containing convalescent rescued plants and decorated randomly with various unusual items from Lydia's collection of oddities such as lovely,

21

contorted Tahitian driftwood and interesting Tibetan stones with marvellously peculiar vibrations, became a place of fascination to the Crew who lingered nonchalantly by the front gate adjusting their bike chains or chaffing each other loudly.

Not, of course, that they appeared to show any interest in Miss Larkin's establishment whatever. That would have contravened the unspoken rule that such behaviour was unseemly and led to a person looking like a dumb kid. So they simply found they accumulated at the end of the Terrace along with the wind-blown petals from the cherry tree in front of Number 19; a drift of blushing faux-snow that had the Crew off their bikes and kicking through the scented whiteness shouting incoherently with joy.

Miss Larkin viewed them from her kitchen window and part of her longed violently to be ten again. Oh, to be a child, unconscious of care, unburdened with knowledge, a blank slate as yet unwritten on by life - but even as she sighed she knew that this vision of un-stained innocence was a fabrication of the Victorian Age (an epoch she deplored - those dresses! So unpleasant to wear) and childhood was not exactly the pure state so many adults would wish it to be. It was as mixed and shadowed as any other part of life - but full of such a questing, unbridled energy that Lydia sighed again as she observed the Crew trying very hard not to be at all bothered about her house - and herself. And for that matter, Hester, with whom she had discussed the children only the day before, after her first close encounter with their captain.

Hester had been sweeping her immaculate front yard with a birch-broom of the traditional type when Joey Delaney had screeched to a halt, stepping off his battered bike and leaving it to fall onto the road, abandoned and without further interest for him until he needed its wonky services again. He gazed levelly at Hester as she swept, and Hester, fully aware of his large, black-lashed hazel-green eyes upon her, calmly continued sweeping as if the tall, skinny ten year old were not there. This delighted Joey, who was more used

22

to being shoo'd, patronised or berated if he encountered adults. This grown-up stuck to the Code - she ignored him, but not in a nasty way, as he put it later to the Crew as they hunched over bags of vilely coloured sweets and bottles of luminous pop in their den, a disintegrating unused unit in the row of ramshackle garages bordering The Terrace.

'She's a witch - proper, honest, she's got the broom thing and all sorts. Her house smells funny too, an' look at the back garden, it looks like a big puzzle effort wotsit.' Joey wiped green sugary dregs from his freckled mouth triumphantly.

Rav, his broad face as placid as ever - despite being a Sikh, his family laughingly called him 'Buddha Baby', sometimes even publicly, to his complete despair - interjected coolly. 'There int no such thing as witches really. Not really. Only on telly, like in 'Charmed' an' stuff. An' The New Ladies are proper old, not like models, like the ones in 'Charmed' so they can't be witches....'

Tiff, one hundred percent loyal to Joey as ever, punched her cousin Rav on the arm scornfully, and a short struggle ensued in which Tiff - despite her gender - got the upper hand quite quickly, and Rav, his pride injured, started to sulk. Tiff was far too athletic and sure of herself for a mere girl, in his opinion; she was quick to punch and kick and she took no prisoners, either. He was about to make a cutting remark about why Tiff should mend her ways and embrace a more conventional femininity, when Joey remarked that they needed to shut their row as he was thinking. A strained silence descended as their leader cogitated.

'Well, they're witches, I reckon - whatever you say, *Buddha Baby*, witches are meant to be old. 'Charmed' is rubbish, it's just for girls. We did stories from around the world last Christmas an' Missus Simms told about Baba Yaga from Russia and she was a right proper witch with steel teeth an' a house that ran after you on giant chicken legs an' she ate kids for breakfast. Baba Yaga is older than your great-granny, Tiff, older than anything, an' The New Ladies aren't that old, they're just pretty old. The one that was sweeping was OK. She didn't go on at me or anything, she was - she was nice.'

Tiff screwed up her face with concentration; thinking bothered her, she was a woman of action, leggy as a colt and with her thick waist-length fall of inky hair braided as tightly as a show-pony. 'But she didn't talk to you. How do you know she were nice?'

Joey grinned triumphantly. 'Because she didn't!' he exclaimed. 'She just kept on with what she was doing but she sort of smiled at the same time. She didn't tell me to go or anything, just swept up her yard. An' her garden's great - you know it is, it's like - like....'

Words failed him and he reflexively prodded Rav who was extremely aggrieved at this two-sided attack and retaliated with his famous kung-fu moves, resulting in a satisfying mass brawl. Finally, exhausted, the Crew lay on the old mattress that was their sofa and wheezed congenially together.

'I was up there this morning,' remarked Tiff casually. 'That blonde one's baking a cake, I could smell it, it were like when my Nan baked, it smelt like that. Good.'

The boys stared at her incredulously. 'You was up there by yourself?' they cried, aghast at her temerity.

Tiff sucked a liquorice stick studded with brilliant pink sugar studs. 'Yeah.'

She was a woman of few words. The boys waited. 'She might give us some. Cake, like. She doesn't have any kids to give it to, so.... She's got a massive black cat too, proper big, like a wild one. It's got yellow eyes. It's called Diane.'

'How do you know?' the boys yelled in unison.

Delighted to be the centre of attention, Tiff paused dramatically. 'Heard her talking to it. Diane, she said, you have to come back tonight you can't be like this forever. It'll be out an' about at night, I reckon, and she's scared it'll get napped like Mrs. Baggot's Cindy. Let's go an' ask her if she wants all that cake for herself or can we have some. I'm starving.'

24

The boys, shocked by this untoward daring and the enormity of Tiff's suggestion, acquiesced silently and, following in her blithe wake, headed up the Terrace to the cake-baking witch and her cat, *Diane*. Only as they reached the gate did the natural order re-assert itself and Joey regain his composure and his leadership.

'I'll knock - I will. You - you just wait an' be ready to run.' He steeled himself, then walked down the short crowded path to the stable-style front door.

Chapter Five

'So I gave them all a cupcake - just some chocolate ones with sugar rosebuds on top and that gold glitter - and they wolfed them down. You'd think they'd never had cake before....'

'I doubt they've ever had cake like *that* before' interjected Hester mildly. 'Most cakes of the bought variety are not made from eighty percent cocoa dark chocolate, garnished with edible flowers and glitter - were they in those gold lamé cases too?'

Lydia tutted. 'Not lamé, silly! Foil. And yes, of course. I was intending them for our soirée that evening but I did a marscapone and blueberry sponge for us instead, do you remember? With the grappa and frozen grapes thing?'

Hester sighed. 'How could I forget? But now those children are quite the regular visitors. Don't you mind? Some would feel it intrusive - didn't the previous owners of your house feel the children were shall we say, déclassé? Personally I am becoming rather an expert on bicycle repair, I found myself pumping up that girl's tyres the other day, and at my time of life. Still, it did rather bring back fond memories of my childhood, cycling round the lanes, free as a proverbial bird. Was the air fresher then, or is that senile of me?'

'Well, a little. But I do think it's all the cars these days, it's not like it was. Do you remember Mount Athos in Spring, my dear? The hyacinth and...'

Hester looked at Lydia quizzically, a forkful of syllabub muffin halfway to her mouth. 'Mount Athos? No, I've never been to Greece, not - no, I haven't. Definitely. For a moment there I thought - it must be your ability to draw one into your memories, Lyddie. Did you go there as a child? I am rather jealous, I have always wanted to travel more, but my family did not approve of foreign jaunts. Amongst other things.'

Lydia bustled unnecessarily round the kitchen, putting the kettle on to boil again and re-arranging perfectly symmetrical tea towels. Hester didn't speak of her family normally, this was a surprising revelation and her concern for her friend drove her embarrassment at her slip about Greece quite out of Lydia's mind. Really, these moments were becoming more frequent - was it Hester who unconsciously unlocked the carefully secured gates of her mind like this? But more importantly, had the children, however déclassé to Glydeminded folk and however importunate regarding bicycle maintenance and cake, opened the iron door of Hester's own childhood a crack? And would the resultant influx of Spring sunlight into that airless place be disinfecting - or disturbing?

'Did they, Hester? Did you never go abroad?'

'Oh goodness, no. That would have been wasteful and indeed, decadent. Sun oil. Garlic. Foreign plumbing. Vulgar types in skimpy bathing costumes. My Father despised that type of thing. He was an academic, as you know. He lived a life of the mind. We had a week at Filey once though, as my mother's step-sister, Aunt Elise, lived a mile or two from the beach. It rained and I sustained a nasty cut on my leg from one of the lumps of metal detritus littering the sands. It had to be stitched and Aunt Elise had hysterics. Father was not pleased. He hated fuss, and we never went away again. He said we should be content with our own home and grateful we had one.'

'Did you mind awfully?'

Hester gazed thoughtfully out of the window at the factory wall, covered in massive swags of Virginia creeper, which shimmered as nesting birds darted in and out of its shaggy safety. Dion sat like an obsidian idol at the foot of this avian tenement, watching intently, his back a study in faux-nonchalance.

'Lyddie, Dion is hunting for the wren again. Did I mind? It paid to say I didn't - my father was not a tolerant man. But yes, if I'm honest, I did rather. The family next door went to Spain, to Andalusia, one year. I watched them preparing, and returning sunburnt and happy, with terracotta planters for the geraniums. They were good enough to bring me a small bronze owl for my collection, I have it still. My father hated them, of course, and their geraniums - he thought them both vulgar beyond words. He didn't know about the owl and I'm afraid I neglected to mention it to him. I heard the parents reminisce when they sat outside on their patio - you can imagine what he thought of that - about the White Towns, the Flamenco, fields of sunflowers and.... Well. It all seemed very romantic to a teenager.'

'Oh Hester - my dear, we could go away somewhere if you liked - we could go to Greece or Spain, flights are very cheap these days and we need not live expensively if you didn't want to. Oh, life is so very short for - for us - and I would so like you to see all the grand old places.'

Hester sneezed loudly, necessitating the use of her handkerchief, one of Mr. Marvell's large, snowy cotton ones embroidered, by Hester, with his initials. This expanse of material served nicely to cover almost her entire face. After a busy moment - while Lydia waited patiently - she emerged somewhat pink and bright-eyed.

'Well, yes, I don't say it wouldn't be nice. I do have a passport. Mr. Marvell insisted just in case - though just in case of what he never explained. Lyddie, could we - do you think we might visit Granada? I understand if you prefer....'

Lydia looked at her friend and felt a great desire to hug her long boniness that had wanted so much and been yoked firmly to her duty first by a tyrant and then by a beloved liberator. But hugs were not Hester, and her business with the handkerchief was as showily emotional as Lydia had ever seen her.

'I shall go to the travel agent tomorrow and get some brochures. Really, I don't know why I didn't think of it before. We'll have a tapas evening and browse Spain. More tea? Oh, I think there's someone at the door - did you hear a - ? Yes, someone's knocking. Will you be so kind as to answer the door, while I....'

And Hester, her head full of oranges and sunshine, did. On the step stood Joey, his great hazel eyes full of unshed tears and blood all over his face.

Chapter Six

In her life with Mr. Marvell - and she thought of her life as having started when she met that gentleman in the reference library where she was working at the time, and he was a borrower of the kind of books that seldom get asked for - Hester Marvell, née Babbige, had quite often had to provide first aid to Mr. Marvell. He had not spared himself in the pursuit of knowledge, and that, as so few know, can be a rigorous, if not downright dangerous game. Hester had dressed burns, bound up sprains, cleaned cuts and - on one memorable occasion - splinted a broken finger with a length of bandage and one of the wooden tongue depressors they used for mixing pastes and unguents. She had quite relished being calm and practical in an emergency, seeing herself as indispensable and coolly nurse-like. Mr. Marvell had been very grateful for her unfussy ministrations and after the finger incident had bought her, as a token of his gratitude, a lovely little silver Victorian Mizpah brooch which she wore most days, even still.

But tending to Mr. Marvell's occasional accidents was quite different, she discovered, from seeing Joey with a black eye obviously swelling and his stark white face, freckles standing out like paint splatter, smeared with glistening still-fresh blood from his snub nose. For a moment Hester gaped at the shivering child, his beloved old skateboard clutched to himself like a teddy-substitute, who stood on Lydia's threshold, silent and helpless.

At the precise moment Lydia called out gaily '*Who is it, dear?*' Hester grabbed her big ashes-of-violets pashmina shawl from the hall coat-hooks and wrapping up the now violently shaking Joey, skateboard and all, bundled him into the kitchen.

Teapot in hand, Lydia turned round with a smile that faded like the sun crossed by a cloud, and as Hester sat the speechless Joey on the nearest chair she rushed to the medicines drawer in the old oak dresser and rummaged around for wound-wash spray and some of the sterile swabs which she had bought to clean up Dion's cut paw a few months previously. Gathering up a clean tea-towel she knelt by the boy, and turned him to face her.

'Joey, Joey - what happened darling? Did you bang your head? Do you hurt anywhere...?'

Joey's intake of breath sounded as if it were coming from the depths of his young being. 'Dave - D-Dave - he....' His eyes were huge in his drawn face and as Lydia deftly wiped the blood from his face silent tears tracked down his cheeks.

As she worked, Lydia gave Hester a look - it meant 'go and get a healing tisane' and Hester didn't need words to understand it. Swiftly she ran next door and brought back a small muslin bundle which she put in a cup with some honey and poured on boiling water. An aromatic steam rose, filling the room with a sweet, refreshing odour. She placed the mug in front of the now more-or-less clean child who sniffed and gulped in a way that tore at her heart. Jaw set, she gathered up the bloody rags and dropped them in the bin, just as Dion moved into the room like a phantom and purred round the lad's shivering legs shaking in their baggy jeans.

Lydia smiled at Joey. 'Look Joey, Dion's come to see if you're alright.'

As Joey glanced at the huge cat and reached out to pet him with a tremulous hand, Lydia moved her fingers behind him in an intricate pattern and the scent of the tisane mixed briefly with a twist of lavender and myrrh while a green shimmer swirled briefly through the air. Hester nodded and smiled at Joey who looked up at her, puzzled but accepting as the pain from his bloodied face and swelling eye faded and a warm feeling of love and acceptance flooded through him. He smiled back gamely.

'Now, who's Dave, my angel? Did you have an accident?' said Lydia gently as Joey continued to pet the uncharacteristically friendly Dion.

'Is this your Diane?' he said in a small voice so unlike his normal boy's shout.

'Diane? Oh, no - he's called Dion, Joey. He's a boy like you.'

'He's dead big, int he? He's not round much though is he? We don't see him like all the other cats. We thought he was called Diane but - Dave's mum's boyfriend, he - he lives at ours now, he - I used his toolkit, to mend my wheels he didn't - he said I weren't to, I know I shouldn't have but I thought he wasn't - he caught me. I was cheeky to him. He said I was. I went to go out an' - he.... I hit my face on the doorframe, I did, I did. Please, Miss, don't tell mum, don't - she'll be mad, she said Dave's her last chance.... I didn't know where else to go, Miss, I didn't - Tiff n' Rav's at a wedding, there int anyone else - an' you.... You give us cake....'

'There, there, don't worry, Hester and I won't say a word if you don't want us to, will we Hester? Will we, Hester - Hester?'

Hester took a deep breath and put away her fury as best she could. 'Of course not, Lydia. Don't worry Joey, just drink some of that tea, it's good for you.'

Gingerly, Joey stopped petting Dion, who looked slightly relieved, and taking hold of the mug sipped cautiously, then drank greedily, only stopping when the mug was empty. Sighing, he put it down and yawned.

Hester and Lydia exchanged glances. 'Come on young man, I think you could do with a nap on the big sofa. That's it - yes, Dion will come too - Dion, Dion - come on now my boys, into the front room.' Lydia's voice had a particular resonance which had even the experienced Hester stifling a yawn as a soft lassitude crept through her. *My goodness*, she thought, *I really must get Lyddie to teach me that one.*

Once Joey was sleeping in the living room with the heavy velvet curtains drawn, propped up on cushions on the big red sofa, still wrapped in Hester's pashmina and covered in the crochet blanket Hester called 'Autumn Days' with Dion curled up by his feet dozing, Lydia and Hester crept back into the kitchen.

Hester had absolutely no expression on her pale face. So much so that her grey eyes seemed almost sightless, and her knuckles, as she gripped the chair back to steady herself, were white. Lydia reflexively put the kettle on. Both women were silent and only the sounds of the house, the gentle creaking and rustlings of an old building, were audible. Hester spoke first, the words issuing from her as if from a long way away.

'I think perhaps we should tell the authorities, the police. That man....'

Lydia sighed. 'Would deny everything. You heard the child. He was running out of the door after a dispute with his stepfather and he tripped and banged his face on the doorframe. The little one will stick with that story come what may - he wants to protect his mother. That - that man -' She paused. 'Hester, better Joey and his friends feel they can come here for sanctuary at any time than we risk alienating his family and being of no use to him whatever. I know - I know, it's not the proper thing to do, but really - I can't - I can't bear the thought of that child feeling there's no place he can go if anything - should happen.'

Lydia put some of her best first flush Darjeeling into the big white teapot, poured in boiling water and added a clove and a cardamom pod. Without thinking she cut the remaining muffin in half and put the halves on white side plates and put them on the table.

'Hester, sit down, my dear. Drink some tea. You know I may not be being very responsible as society today sees it, but I am doing what I think is best. You must do as you think best, of course.'

Hester sat down slowly. Her back was as stiff and straight as a spear. 'Lyddie, I - oh. I know what you're saying. Very well, but if it happens again, we really must....'

A knock at the front door made both women jump and nearly spill their tea. They looked at each other, and Hester raised an eyebrow. They both knew the other was thinking - *Is it the man who hurt Joey?* Hester's jaw set, and Lydia seemed to glow with an inner fire that Hester had never seen before. She suddenly looked not warm and cuddly as usual, but charged with an inner strength that surprised her friend; she seemed to have grown in stature and power, radiating an authority Hester would not have thought possible in such a feminine woman.

The knock sounded again and Lydia got up, walked to the door, and opened it. Hester braced herself to see the vile bully who had beaten a defenceless boy.

But instead, a thin, short, dark-haired woman stood outside, nervously twisting the hem of her pale blue fleece jacket in her hands, her long acrylic nails lacquered a chemical peach and decorated with rhinestones, a strange elaboration at odds with her worn, un-made-up face.

'Excuse me, is Joey here? I'm his mum, Lyn, Lyn Delaney. My - my fella said he's had an accident, like, and Bob Baggot said he saw him run up here like they do now, bothering you ladies - is he here?'

Lydia stepped back, the strange version of herself vanished, the old Lyddie, warm and fragrant, returned.

'Won't you come in, Mrs. Delaney? Joey is here, he's just sleeping, he had rather a shock, I'm afraid, he....'

Hester could see the woman bridling. 'No, well, I'm very sorry he come an' annoyed you, really. He's a proper handful, it's always something. Runs us ragged, let me tell you. He's nothing but trouble, like his father. I'm at my wit's end, I really am. I'm on pills because of him, and the way he goes on. I'll take him home now, if you can just get him - sleeping? Why is he sleeping?' Mrs. Delaney looked suddenly puzzled as if Lydia's words had only just sunk in, her rambling narrative interrupted by a concept she could not understand.

'Please, come in Mrs. Delaney. Hester, pour Mrs. Delaney some tea - no, it's no trouble, really, we were just having some ourselves. This is my friend and neighbour, Mrs. Marvell. I am Mrs. Larkin, Lydia Larkin, please call me Lydia. Would you like some cake, or a biscuit?'

Lyn Delaney sat at the table and Hester watched her eyes wander round the kitchen as if she had never seen its like before, which no doubt, she hadn't. Through her astonishment Hester saw anew the old polished wood floor, the exposed brick of the chimney breast supporting the odd gilt-framed, Venetian mirror, the little wood-burning stove and the big cream Aga. She realised that, to Mrs. Delaney, the bunches of herbs hanging from the drying rack along with the copper pans and some pretty blue worry beads, the battered oak dresser loaded with mis-matched china and a small carved bone skull set with amber, the Tiffany dragonfly-pattern pendant lamp and the long, old pine table at which she sat represented another world, an unknown and possibly dangerous world and that to Mrs. Delaney, she and Lydia were two middle-aged madwomen, possibly lesbians as there were no men in view, and certainly, as she would have it, hippie weirdoes.

She put her hands in her lap and wove a long, complex pattern with her fingers. Lydia, sensing immediately what she was doing, smiled and asked the bemused Mrs. Delaney if she would care for sugar, or perhaps some milk?

The air suffused with the soft and lovely fragrance of ylang-ylang and oud, while a sound, barely audible, of silvery bells chimed then faded as gold iridescence gleamed round the light overhead.

Mrs. Delaney sighed. She sipped her milkless, sugarless tea, which normally she would have called proper nasty, and years of bitterness and conflict with a world she saw as set against her fell from her face, revealing the small, delicate features of the girl she once was. The hard black of her dyed hair seemed to soften to the lustrous dark brown of her youth and a pink flush heightened her pallid complexion. If only, Hester thought, the physical effects were permanent, then perhaps the foul Dave would not be this tired creature's last chance. But she knew that whilst Mrs. Delaney's sense that the two ladies at the end of the cul-de-sac were nice, harmless - if rather eccentric - arty types, would be permanent, the look of regained youth would fade in a few hours. The effort of such a difficult Glamour tired her and she realised she had not been listening to the conversation.

'... I do like your air freshener, is it one of them plug-ins, it smells lovely. Joey says you bake your own cakes, I wish I could but I never could get the hang of it myself and I just don't have the time. My mum, now she could bake, but it's proper gone out of fashion, hasn't it? This is nice tea, is it a herbal one? Very spicy.'

'Yes, we like it - now, Joey....' Lydia poured more tea for Mrs. Delaney, whose softened face looked rather more like her son's than it had when she'd first come in. But as for Joey's cleft chin, his large, almond-shaped greeney-hazel eyes, his roughly waving copper-brown hair, his length of limbs - all those must have come from his absent father. Dead, or run away? wondered Hester. Bolted, she decided uncharitably. Oh, definitely bolted.

'Joey?' Mrs. Delaney looked momentarily puzzled as if she had never heard her son's name before. Hester reminded herself not to be quite so effective with the rejuvenatory properties of that particular Glamour in future. Youthfulness was one thing, amnesia quite another.

'Joey - your son? He's ....' Lydia said gently.

'Oh - yeah, him. Oh, I don't mind telling you, he's a proper burden to me that kid. Ever since his dad run off....'

Hester allowed herself a small, almost invisible, smile.

'Ever since that he's been a proper handful - cheeky! My god, you wouldn't believe the stuff he comes out with! Course, he hero-worshipped his dad - well, he didn't know him like I did. He could do no wrong for Joey but with me - you mustn't do this, you mustn't do that - no going out with my friends to the club, no drinking - as if I were some kind of nun or something! Course he's a Catholic, Irish, proper had the gift of the gab as they say, and proper good-looking. Joey takes after him, dead spit. At least he couldn't say he weren't his kid - he looks that like him. I suppose that don't help with Dave - they were mates y'see. That's how I come to know him. Dave's been a tower of strength to me, he's my rock, really. He's got his problems, who doesn't? I mean, he can be quick tempered, and he likes a drink, it's true - but Joey don't need to give him such lip all the time, I mean, Dave's my - well, you know, I'm not getting no younger, none of us is, eh?'

'Oh, indeed, no, very true. Ah - does Dave ever - well - discipline Joey?' Lydia said carefully.

Mrs. Delaney looked confused. 'Discipline? Oh - you mean like does he tick him off and that? Well of course. He's not a man to take cheek off a kiddie, he's got his standards, like he says. I mean, a clip round the ear never hurt no-one, and kids these days! But he never proper hurt him, oh no, he wouldn't do that. Why do you ask? What's that little bas - what's Joey been saying? Oh, I could wring his neck the way he tells lies and says stuff, I really could, I....'

Hester put a plate of Lydia's chocolate biscotti down in front of Mrs. Delaney rather more firmly than was required. 'No reason, none at all. Joey told us he'd tripped and fallen as he ran out of the door. No doubt he was rather dazed and confused, perhaps even slightly concussed. That's why he came here. And really, it's no trouble for us to care for him. He's a very polite child, most courteous.'

Mrs. Delaney automatically ate a piece of biscotti. 'Bit dry these. Are they foreign? I love them Hobnobs myself. Joey? Polite? Well, an angel in the street and a devil in the house as they say. I don't doubt he'll be alright with you, trying to make a good impression, he does it at school, too, always sucking up to the teachers. His Mrs. Simms! Oh, you'd think the sun shone out of her ar - her behind, you would. You don't have kids then, Mrs....'

'Marvell. Hester Marvell. No, I'm afraid I don't. I'm a widow.'

'Oh, shame. And you neither, Mrs. Larkin? No. Well, you're better off that way, trust me. Nothing but trouble. Now, I'll not bother you no more, I'll get him off home....'

'I'll just fetch him for you - no, it's fine.' Hester hurried from the room, her face averted from Joey's mother.

Mrs. Delaney watched her go out of the room with a pitying expression on her face. Then she turned confidentially to Lydia and smoothed down her hair with a work-reddened hand on which the plastic nails sat like eagle's talons. Lydia wondered why someone who so obviously had to work with her hands chose to submit to having such impractical appendages glued to her fingers. Glamour, she thought. The other kind, not our kind. The desire for beauty can be a savage tyrant, she mused. Foot-binding, corsets, cerusse, breast implants, stiletto heels, the list is endless. Beauty demands sacrifices, offerings of pain, impossible hopes and delusion. And for what? Men? Bless them, they never notice these things, they just like a warm, sweetly fragrant armful of bosom, bottom and comfort. And certainly not inch-long acrylic claws painted a very curious shade of metallic orange and decorated with diamanté. How on earth did the woman do up her clothes, or pick up anything small?

Mrs. Delaney nodded her head at the door Hester had just exited through, 'Well, she's a rum one, isn't she? No offence, with her being your friend and all. But a bit of a schoolmarm, isn't she? Well thank you everso for looking after Joey, I'll make sure he don't bother you ladies again, I'll give him such a....'

Lydia said quickly, 'Really, he's no bother, none at all. We rather enjoy his company, and the other children. As you say, we have no children ourselves so it's quite pleasant for us to have them round to play. Of course, with your permission, naturally.'

'Well, if you put it like that - I don't mind, I'm sure.' Mrs. Delaney bridled and looked gratified. How many people had ever asked her permission about anything? thought Lydia, sadly. We are all the children of happenstance, the hostages of fate, as Gyremandel said. Indeed, she sighed inwardly. And none more so than this poor, foolish woman.

At that moment Hester brought a sleepy Joey into the kitchen. His swollen eye was considerably reduced due to the combination of the tisane and Lydia's ministrations, and he looked much less white and shocked. His thick hair stood on end in a series of cowlicks and his skateboard trailed from his hand.

'Mum - what - I....'

Mrs. Delaney stood, and in a swift practised gesture took hold of the boy by the arm, starting to drag him towards the door when she stopped with a little scream. Dion had slipped round from behind Joey and was standing between her and the door, his hackles raised and his tail bottle-brushed. A few sparks flew out of his shining fur, noticed only by Lydia and Hester.

Mrs. Delaney stood aghast, clutching Joey until he winced as her nails bit through his t-shirt. 'Ooh! That cat - it give me a proper fright - it's massive, like a bloody dog - is it safe? I don't like cats, me - sneaky devils - go on, shoo!'

Dion looked calmly at Joey, his great yellow eyes unblinking. Joey smiled at him wanly. 'Don't, Mum, that's Dion, Mrs. Lydia's cat. He's a pedigree, he won't hurt you, come on. Sorry Mrs. Lydia, sorry Dion.'

Dion moved out of the way like the night air sighing through a dark cypress tree and cast a look of freezing disdain at Mrs. Delaney. In turn, Lydia's expression caused him to sit on his daybed and take an inordinate interest in cleaning his right front paw.

When their visitors had left, Hester and Lydia looked at each other in silence, because they both felt nothing they could say would be adequate, and if they did say something, it might well involve a great deal of what Hester's grandmother had always called 'sailor's language'. Then they both returned to their separate studies, Lydia to work on a little treatise she was putting together on the influence of mandrake and trance-inducing ritual dancing on early Lithuanian religious practices, after which she felt she might do some work on her new painting, and Hester to mix up a batch of her Marvell's Attar Of Roses Purification Cream for the relief of rashes, wrinkles and lack of confidence. It was her most popular unguent and orders came from around the world. At least the street would smell beautiful for a few hours.

Chapter Seven

The summer, an unusually pleasant one with much sunshine and refreshing showers that always seemed to fall in the early hours of the morning and vanish with the dawn, proceeded without any repetition or mention of the incident that had brought Joey to the ladies' door in such distress. The gardens all along the cul-de-sac enjoyed a very fruitful season which caused the estimable Mr. Baggot to remark on more than one occasion that it was quite like the old days, as if the old days were a cornucopia of everything fertile and good. But that was how the little community behind the high factory wall felt. Peace and tranquility reigned undisturbed and the days were long, warm and golden, hazy and thrumming with bees, as if the street were in a bucolic country village rather than a mere two miles from the urban cacophony of the town centre, where, were the local media to be believed, the city was sinking into the depths of depravity at an alarming rate. The Express & Clarion, or the E&C as it was more familiarly known, printed increasingly inflammatory editorials about the lack of moral fibre and the younger generation's inability to engage with higher personal and spiritual issues - this alongside stringer stories from the national press about scantily-attired American actresses' love-lives. It all seemed very distant from the street, as if somehow the little row of houses had been transported to a parallel universe where people liked each other and neighbours lent each other cups of sugar or their lawnmower without considering litigation when it was not returned promptly enough for their tastes.

Joey, Rav and Tiff were at Lydia and Hester's most days, sometimes for a few minutes, sometimes for hours. They drew on sheets of sugar paper Lydia used for her sketches - and she sketched them over and over much to their delight. Lydia was always able to catch a likeness, and her deft little chalk pastel pictures of the children were charming. She sent a portrait sketch of each of the children to their respective parents - Tiff and Rav's families were effusive in their thanks, thrilled by a 'real picture' of their offspring and had the drawings framed, much to Rav's discomfiture and Tiff's intense pride. According to Rav she would make a point, when visitors came, of lingering by the picture in an artistic attitude, or as he put it 'like a right drip'. From Joey's mother there wasn't a word. Later Lydia found out Mrs. Delaney had simply dropped the sketch on the table from where it fell on the floor and Dave trod on it. Joey had rescued the picture, complete with size ten boot-print, and kept it under his bed in his Memory Box, an idea first started by his father, and which was stuffed with all his small treasures. A ticket stub and programme for a Manchester United game his father had taken him to; photographs; a broken pocket-knife of his father's; and string. Joey was big on string.

At the same time, Hester was building up something of a devoted clientele for her unguents and lotions. It had started with Tiff's mother, Sandra, who had, in a mad moment, booked two sessions on a sunbed within twenty-four hours to 'prepare herself' for her forthcoming holiday in Cyprus. Tiff had mentioned to Lydia and Hester - in that falsely casual way children have when they're concerned - that her mum was 'proper fried' and suffering both from the effects of the sunbed and Tiff's father Jazwinder making bluff, manly remarks about Sandra resembling a well-done sirloin. Hester had despatched Tiff post haste with a jar of Marvell's Attar Of Roses Purification Cream and a bottle of Marvell's Aloe And Sandalwood Calming Lotion. Such was the effect, that young Mrs. Singh, née Appleton, appeared sobbing with gratitude on Hester's doorstep, her complexion fully restored to its original creamy loveliness. Then it was Mrs. Baggot's infamous rash, notoriously untouched by all the various ministrations of modern medical science and a considerable burden to her in the warm weather. It succumbed almost instantly to Marvell's Spike Lavender Healing & Cooling Balm and after this triumph, verging on the miraculous in the eyes of the women of the little community who had been receiving bulletins about the progress of the rash from Mrs. Baggot for years, a small but steady stream of ladies consulted Hester on such feminine mysteries as crêpe throat, red knuckles, ragged cuticles, cellulite, stretch-marks, hot flushes, thread veins and the ever present sense of not quite being up to par and feeling their physical appearance did not correspond with the current feminine ideal.

Hester was careful never to over-step the bounds. Although she could have prescribed a number of particularly efficacious mixtures and compounds, she had no wish to be thought of as a rival to the local medical community. She knew only too well from Mr. Marvell's early struggles, how protective they could be of their territory. So she stuck to her creams and lotions, which could be considered simply cosmetic, merely enhancing them with small charms and ensuring they were effective and pleasant to use. She often thought the esoteric formulae and ancient rituals she used to produce them were not a patch on the fact they smelt gorgeous and felt like silk. This naturally made her sigh, but she was pleased that she had brought some relief to women suffering from what was, at heart, really low self-esteem more than anything else. Hester herself did not suffer from either low or high self-esteem. She trod the middle path, as recommended by numerous sages through the millenia. It was, she felt, the only sensible way.

So the summer proceeded and Lydia and Hester baked, stirred, macerated, embroidered, sketched, gardened, and on one memorable occasion had a make-your-own-pizza party in Lydia's garden for the children when they discovered none of them could cook anything from scratch. This resulted in Hester and Lydia being presented with fancy aprons from Rav's mother's catalogue as a thank you gift - Hester's was black and bore the slogan 'Domestic Goddess'; Lydia's, pink and patterned with cup-cakes. They were both secretly thrilled with these evidences of affection and although Hester made acerbic remarks she wore the apron almost constantly.

Other exciting things happened, such as an owl taking up residence in the enormous old ash tree at the bottom of Hester's garden and hooting in a sepulchral manner at night, and Dion narrowly escaped being run over by Dave's van one misty morning. Lydia suspected Dion was watching over Joey in his own, mysterious fashion and for his own, equally mysterious reasons, but on questioning him, received only an enigmatic topaz stare. Hester opined that Dion could perfectly well understand all that was being said to him, and Lydia agreed but added severely that if he did, he wouldn't let on. Dion merely yawned enormously, displaying the red ribbed interior of his mouth and a fine set of ivory fangs.

Then one day, Lydia heard her letter-box clang and found a folded paper lying on her mat. Glancing out of the kitchen window she saw Mrs. Delaney hurrying away from Hester's door, dragging a miserable-looking Joey with her, and marching up the Baggots' yard where she posted something through their door. Shortly afterwards, Hester appeared, dressed as a Domestic Goddess, with a thoughtful expression on her face and her reading glasses round her neck on their antique silver chain.

'By the pricking of my thumbs, something wicked this way comes' she intoned. 'Have you read this?'

Lydia had not. She unfolded the luridly coloured paper to discover it was an advertisement. A banner headline in bright yellow on a red background read, 'ARE YOU UNHAPPY? DO YOU FEEL HOPELESS?'

Lydia felt a frisson of apprehension which exceeded that which she might have expected from merely reading a flyer. She continued.

RAY LOKEY WILL TAKE YOUR TROUBLES AWAY! AS SEEN ON TV! INTERNATIONALLY FAMOUS SPIRITUAL LEADER **RAY LOKEY** AUTHOR OF BOOKS SUCH AS 'BEYOND GOD' AND 'THE BUSY PERSON'S PATH TO ENLIGHTENMENT' AND PRESENTER OF POPULAR CABLE TV PROGRAMME **'PRAY WITH RAY'** WILL LEAD A SPIRITUAL REVIVAL IN YOUR TOWN!!!!!! SEE LOCAL PRESS FOR DETAILS OR LOG ON TO **WWW. PRAYWITH-RAY.COM**. RAY SAVES! THIS IS _YOUR_ CHANCE TO BE _EVERYTHING_ YOU WANT TO BE AND _MORE_!!!!!

Beneath this, a small box was wonkily over-printed with the legend: 'Meet And Pray With Ray At The Bountiful Haven Life Church, Hartley Bank Road. Every day (except Mondays) at 7.00 pm (prompt).' Underneath were a pair of rather grainy photographs of a pretty young blonde - 'Miss Sam Price, Model' - looking first wistful, then elated and captioned 'Before' and 'After' with the ringing endorsement that the young woman in question had been feeling 'very low', her life 'going nowhere' before she 'prayed with Ray' after which she became a successful model featured in national newspapers. And also a florist. '_And I owe it all to Ray Lokey - the modern day prophet for Our Times. If you want a better life, don't delay! Pray with Ray!_'

Lydia read the ridiculous endorsement and felt as if the world had suddenly become monochrome, while a slithery chill wrapped her in a clammy serpentine embrace. The whole pathetic advertisement was obviously for a ridiculous sham designed, no doubt, to extract money from the desperate and credulous, but - where had she heard that name before? Ray Lokey - she knew it, she - there was a vibration attached to the sound of the syllables, a tiny but quite effective controlling device set to draw the mind in - Ray Lokey - where had she heard that name, felt that vibration ....

'…and, if I may say so, a most promiscuous use of exclamation points. That never bodes well, to my mind. Lyddie - Lydia, you're not listening to me - Lyddie, are you alright? You look - sit down, do you feel faint?'

'No dear, I…'

Lydia turned the cheap shiny paper over. On the reverse was a full page studio photograph titled 'Ray Lokey - Spiritual Leader'. Lydia studied the face that gazed back at her with such studied benevolence. Ray Lokey bore, to her mind, quite a resemblance to the actor, Kirk Douglas, when young. A similar triangular structure with high, sharp cheekbones narrowing to a chiselled chin marked with a deep dimple. Thin but well-shaped lips. Strongly marked eyebrows tilted slightly upwards over beautiful almond-shaped eyes which, despite the black and white photograph, showed pale and glacial. Thick, rather long hair sprung back from a widow's peak on a low, broad forehead. The ears were neat, small and placed high on a round skull. At one point they had obviously (to Lydia at least) been pierced for earrings, as a tiny dark hole remained in each narrow lobe. It was a commanding face, archaic and mask-like even, not a modern face at all. It was a face that did not brook opposition; it looked fox-like, cunning and intelligent. Very intelligent indeed. And, to Lydia, very familiar - if only she could remember just where she had seen it before.

It was also, like the name, set within a small but very effective Enticing Glamour that wove a neat little lure before dissipating into a slight but definite longing to see this handsome fox-face in the flesh. To be guided by the wisdom that emanated from those arctic eyes.…

Mr. Lokey was obviously a force to be reckoned with.

'Lydia - Lydia - what is it?' There was a note of distress in Hester's voice that recalled Lydia to herself. Hester's face was white and strained, and she was clutching the fabric of her apron in her hand, the material bunched tight. 'You look - different. What is it? Who is this man?'

Lydia glanced at herself in the mirror and hurriedly re-arranged her expression. 'I'm not sure, dear. I thought I recognised him but from where, I can't say. Hester, there's a Glamour on this flyer. One in the photograph and another weaker one in the text. Whoever Mr. Lokey is, he knows his stuff.'

Hester automatically put the kettle on to boil. 'Yes, I felt something, very drawing - I can't imagine what that would do if you weren't - well, if you weren't like us. Mrs. Delaney, for example. I saw her when she posted this thing through my letterbox, she looked quite a different person from the one we spoke to when Joey - had his accident. She had the boy with her. He looked most unhappy. *She* looked like a person with a purpose in life. I hesitate to use the word, but she looked….'

'Possessed?' said Lydia, wearily.

Hester filled the tea pot and set it down on the table by a blue glass vase full of lupins and damask roses. She sat down opposite Lydia and poured her a cup then pushed it across to her, the steam wreathing the flowers and drawing forth a faint ghost of their essential perfumes which mingled with the beautiful scent of the black rose-petal china tea.

'Well, yes' said Hester. 'I hate that word - so debased by Hollywood.' Hester pronounced the word 'Hollywood' with shrivelling contempt. 'I try not to use the word, or indeed the commonly perceived concept, but…'

Lydia sighed. 'But we both know what the real thing actually is. The beaten woman crawling back to her abuser, unable to resist, unable even to explain why she does it. The woman married to a killer who washes his blood-stained clothes and gives him an alibi because she thinks she loves him. The religious fanatic who murders little children in the name of faith because he's been told by his leaders such children are witches. The - oh, the list is endless. They are possessed. Not by demons, but by ideas, by the power of another person's mind - charisma, now there's another mis-used word and concept. Now they apply it to singers and entertainers, or politicians, when what they really want to say is that those people are good at performing on the stage. Hester, this Ray Lokey - I hesitate to seem overly dramatic, but…'

'You think he's dangerous.' Hester's slim, shapely lips were compressed into a tight line. Her dark brows drew level over storm cloud grey eyes. To Lydia, what Hester really was seemed so obvious, especially when she was angry or disturbed, yet Hester was seemingly oblivious. How, thought Lydia, could she not remember? Could the past be so very deeply buried? So much time had passed since they had all made their decisions, but surely even a Cellular Restructuring Glamour would have worn off by now? How glad she was she had opted to remain herself, despite heartbreak, despite the years of wandering, the loves lost, the sorrows. She had felt such joy, seen such beauty, loved so marvellously. And love was what she had been made for, after all - love of all sorts. Hester, though, was a warrior-maid. The cool armour of logic and intelligence clothed her and though her passion was contained it was no less fiery for that. Her stormy eyes always sought the truth, the essence, the heart of the matter. Hester was a spear, straight and true. One could always depend on her.

Lydia toyed with her cup. 'Yes. I believe he's dangerous and much more than he seems. Hester, I think we should pay Mr. Lokey a visit. Are you willing to accompany me? It might be - well, it might not be very pleasant. He might be rather a nasty character, under all that - yes, indeed, under that charm.'

Hester reached out and took hold of Lydia's hand. 'I don't want to think of our boy mixed up in anything like this, Lyddie. Mrs. Delaney is an adult, but Joey - he looked so distressed. Lydia, I am more than happy to accompany you. To the Gates Of Hell, if needful. Or indeed, The Bountiful Haven Life Church.'

Chapter Eight

Dion came home late. The night was balmy and a faint breeze stirred the coral-coloured Thai silk curtains in Lydia's bedroom, setting the crystal drops of the old chandelier shivering. Lydia heard the clacka-clack of the dog door (Dion was too big for a cat flap) opening and closing, and the heavy pad of Dion climbing the stairs. Then the bed creaked with the weight of the huge cat as he settled in his accustomed place next to her. His purring vibrated like a steam engine, she felt him stretching luxuriously and smelt the ozone of the night air in his fur.

'Dion, how long is this going to go on? Will you be like this forever?' Lydia said in a low voice, sitting up and pulling her peach silk peignoir trimmed with antique Alencon lace closer around her. She never wore a proper nightgown but preferred to sleep in a kimono - of which she had a very artistic selection from her trips to Japan - or a wrap. Although a nightgown might be more practical in an emergency, she disliked the constriction and had always thought a charming dishabille was the most attractive option, even if fleeing fire or flood. Hester on the other hand, had a nun-like black fleece dressing gown of her own manufacture that buttoned severely to the neck, had book-sized pockets usually stuffed with tomes, and extended in severe folds to her black sheepskin mule-shod feet. Her nightgowns, she averred, were her own concern. She had offered to construct a dressing gown - 'a sensible one' - for Lydia and had been somewhat affronted at that lady's giggles.

So Lydia sat in her big bed, wrapped in silk and lace and studying the great cat beside her. Oh Dion, she thought, what shall I do with you?

The dim light in the room seemed to shift subtly into an opalescent haze and the air filled with the scent of mountain thyme and hyacinth. Lydia looked across at the black cat to see his outlines shift and twist for a second in a way that confounded the mind and transcended the natural order of the world, or would if you weren't used to it as Lydia was; even so, she shivered as the sound of bees and a soughing wind coiled past her.

Then, where the black cat had lain, was a young male leopard, his coruscating emerald eyes, pupils a black thread, regarding Lydia calmly and his shimmering golden spotted coat gleaming molten in the half light. Lydia could feel his hot breath on her arm, see the ivory fangs in his parted mouth, feel the weight of him against her side. She smelt his strong, feral, but not unpleasant, odour. She was not afraid. She had no reason to be.

'Dion, please. Yes, you are very beautiful and yes, I love you to distraction, but my dear, this is no time for games.'

She tried to sound stern, but the leopard, who would have sent most people screaming out of the door in utter terror, butted her and rubbed his shining head against her, soliciting a delicious back-of-the ear scratch. Sighing, Lydia gave in to him and rubbed the thick fur behind the mobile ears. Then she took one of the huge paws in her soft hands and spread the hooked claws out from the calloused pads, like sabres springing from velvet.

'We have a problem, my love. I fear greatly one of the Old Ones has come to our little sanctuary, and he is not, I feel, benevolent. Dion - Dion - come back to me, I need to speak with you.'

And in a whirling nanosecond, sitting cross-legged on the bed was a naked youth, a wreath of vine leaves in his mass of coppery black curls, his long, narrow dark-sapphire eyes those of something wild you might glimpse on a hillside. His skin was tanned and silken, his slim, muscular frame that of a youth of nineteen - but one glimpse into those slanting eyes showed age beyond reckoning. A boy he might look, but there was something unearthly strange about him. Those who would have been terrified of the leopard, would have fainted dead away at the sight of the boy, radiating animal power and archaic wildness, sitting nonchalantly on Lydia's bed, a hieratic half-smile curving his full red lips.

'Euoi - I am, as ever, at your command, my Queen' he said, in a dialect long-forgotten and not pronounced on this earth for thousands of years. The strange cadences filled Lydia's heart with a bitter-sweet longing and nostalgia, and she replied in the same language.

'How happy I am to see you again, my lord. I have missed your presence in this guise very much - it has been some time since you appeared to me so.'

The youth toyed with a tassle on the velvet throw. 'Yes, I know. But time has little meaning for me now, to tell the truth. Oh beautiful one, I tire of this modern world, the noise and crowds - so crude, so ignorant of anything of real value. Everywhere now stinks of their effluent, their machines. Even the wild hillsides we roamed laughing in the white sun are filled with their leavings, and shrill with the sounds of their din. Were it not for you, my love, I would have long since retired to the other place. But while you tarry, so do I - will you not consider leaving these mortals? Surely by now, you have had enough of their petty, destructive lives?'

Lydia sighed. 'You were never very interested in them, Dion. They were merely toys for your whims, and their passions and panics were your amusements. That was your role, to remind them of what is wild and savage in nature and themselves, to show them ecstasy and trance. But I - that was not my task, my duties lay elsewhere as you know - and I cannot bear to leave them. I feel so sorry for them, they need more than ever to know the value and necessity of love, and who will teach them if I go? But even I tire, I admit it. I sometimes feel as if they want to destroy themselves despite our best efforts. I thought myself blessed when I found this place and what it holds, and recently I….'

'Recently, beloved?'

'I feel a great urge to go, as you said, to the other place. And I would have, *we* would have, my love, had I not met Hester, who does not know who she is, and the boy-child, Joey, whom you have been guarding, my lord - yes, I know you have.'

The youth stretched and put out his hand to the side table. Where there was a plain glass of water before, now appeared a shallow-bowled, black, two-handled cup on a short pedestal base decorated inside with a stylised dancing figure in terracotta-colour. Lydia knew the cup well. It had been her favourite in those far off days when she and Dion had been young and carefree in their power and in the glory of their laughing days. Dion knew she had liked the cup and had richly rewarded the artist who had made it - his bones now long dust in the wind. Smiling, Dion passed his hand over the cup and it filled with dark, resinous wine, purplish, blood-deep and heavy. The scent of it alone was intoxicating; it spoke of dark pine trees on sun-hot hillsides, the purple sea curling onto jewel-like bays guarded by tumbling falls of ochre crags and little stark white temples set against skies of numinous blue. It was wine that would have left a normal person drunk merely from inhaling that dizzying, exquisite aroma, their mind filled with visions of the fertile earth's slow ripening into the grapes that bore this vintage. This wine, glowing in the old cup, had been not been pressed within the living memory of the oldest of the old, or indeed, their great-great-great-great grandmother. It was Chian wine, from a distant and mythic past, and its like had never been seen in the world again.

Dion picked up the cup, drank, and passed it to Lydia who sighed, but sipped some too. The strange wine stained the youth's full lips an even darker red, and flushed his smooth, high-boned cheeks with rose. In the incalculable depths of his azure eyes, light danced like the sun on a summer sea, prismatic and coruscating like diamonds. He was immensely uncanny; his youthful beauty and apparent relaxed ease shockingly contrasting with the wickedly sharp glitter of those ancient eyes. Lydia leant over and kissed the proffered cheek. It felt like satin and smelt deliciously of apricots warmed by the sun. How she loved him. Of her many loves, mortal and immortal, none compared to this wild boy, none had ever thrilled her as he did, even after the myriad of their lifetimes together. Yet he was no husband to her, nor would he have even understood what that meant. He was as feral as the cats he loved to become, as disinterested in habit and domesticity as a mountain puma. Perhaps, thought Lydia languorously, that's why I love him: he is so purely and completely what he is. And very distracting.

'You didn't answer me, Dion. Why do you watch the child? It is unlike you to care about such a one.'

Dion moved closer to Lydia and ran his finger down her arm, ruffling the fine silk. 'You love him, Queen. He is unprotected and has no-one to train him to survive and live with honour. His mother is an empty vessel waiting to be filled with whatever her light virtue craves. The man she lives with is a weakling and a bully. I have seen those faces a thousand, thousand times....' Dion gazed at Lydia, his head tilted on one side. 'That you care at all for the child, beloved, means you have seen what he might be, what he could grow towards. And I also see something yearning in his human heart, something that could be noble, after his kind. I have often thought it was a very sad thing that one made for love, like you, should be denied motherhood. So I do some small service to you by watching over the boy in the night when he is most vulnerable. I would greatly prefer just to kill both the mother and her lover, then you could raise him as a fosterling - but do not fear. I know, my lady, that those days are past. Sadly.' Dion smiled reflectively and putting his arm round Lydia drew her to him and kissed her again, this time on the lips.

As Lydia returned the kiss the room filled with the scent of tea roses. A veil of sparkling golden mist swirled round the pair as they lay entwined and they were both in the room and in a place out of time and space. Outside, the Aurora Borealis flickered briefly in an English night sky.

Their lovemaking, as fresh and sweet as dawn, was also a ritual as old as time itself and it renewed the earth as it pleased them. Afterwards, Dionysus and Aphrodite lay on the big iron bed, in a little bedroom in an undistinguished suburb of a small provincial city, and talked of the old days and their old companions. They fell asleep, wrapped in each other's arms as a gentle shower pattered down outside. And all over the world, fresh shoots and tender buds appeared, green and fertile; animals quickened; sleepy young women lovingly patted their swollen bellies full of the longed-for child while their men felt the painfully sweet rush of fatherly pride; and lovers sighed and kissed in an ecstasy of passion.

And across the city, in the only smart, expensive hotel there was in town, a creature who had taken the shape of a human man stirred and then sat upright suddenly in his white-sheeted bed in his blandly modern room. His light blue eyes roiled with a cold fire as brutal as ice floes sweeping down a freezing fjord. Yes, the creature cried aloud, *yes* - I knew it, I knew it. All I need is here, here of all the places on earth - who would have thought it? Who would have felt that pull but me? Oh, clever, *clever* me - I will triumph! I *will*. And the thing chuckled at his own brilliance then lay back and closed his eyes as if asleep, while the night turned chilly with a cold sharp wind coming down from the far North.

Chapter Nine

'D'you know, Lyddie,' said Hester as they sat on her swing seat drinking homemade lemonade, 'I believe we had a small earthquake last night. I woke and my room definitely juddered. Really, this is becoming more and more common, you'd think we lived in foreign climes, not England. We have rain, not earthquakes, this is not California. And talking of rain, last night's shower has definitely perked up my herbs, look, they've put out new shoots since yesterday - but I must say I think it's turned rather chilly. I hope we're not in for one of those cold spells we get occasionally, it's such a shame when it's been so lovely. Oh, you've spilt your drink - did it go down the wrong way? Do you need a tissue?'

Hester looked virtuous - as she always did when she talked about the weather, or gardening, in what she considered the proper, decorous manner - and handed Lydia a paper napkin printed with bats and skulls (left over from the previous Halloween) from the tray. Lydia, pink-cheeked and coughing, was trying to ignore Dion who had winked at her as he strolled past during the mention of earthquakes. She smiled gamely at Hester who looked quizzical - but then, Hester generally looked quizzical, so that was no indication that she knew more than she said or, indeed, that she had seen Dion winking.

'Ah - well - was there? I can't say I noticed, but I slept rather heavily, I must say. Hmm, yes - but you said you wanted to talk about something, dear? I mean, presumably not just the weather?'

Hester gazed into the cloudless sky that sat like a luminous blue dome above them and smoothed her Domestic Goddess apron across her lap. She sighed, and tucked her silvery hair behind her ear with an absent gesture. Obviously, there was something on her mind.

'Lyddie,' Hester sighed even more heavily, then recovering herself began again. 'Lyddie, you know I'm not given to extremes. I try never to be angry or indeed, overly elated. I strive to maintain a steady course through life. I take great comfort from the teachings of such masters as Marcus Aurelius or our dear Gyremandel. I have read the Meditations Of Mistress Lilliard from beginning to end, repeatedly. These sages speak of stoicism, of maintaining a middle way. I - I...'

'Yes, dear?'

'I am ashamed to say it, but I am having great difficulty restraining myself from marching down to Mrs. Delaney's house and smacking her face. There, I said it. No doubt you think less of me. I certainly think less of myself. But the damned woman is making our boy's life a misery. Dear little Tiffany was here just before you came, and the poor child was near to tears. Joey is no longer allowed to play with her and their other friends in case they "contaminate" him.'

Hester made quote marks in the air around the word "contaminate". That she used the word *damned* was an indication of her extreme distress. Lydia had never heard her swear, however mildly, before. Lydia examined her friend's face. That she was righteously angry did not surprise Lydia: Hester was a warrior nun, a shield maiden committed to the pursuit of knowledge, truth and justice. Those level grey eyes would indeed be formidable to the wrongdoer. Lydia sighed: It was beginning. Much more quickly than she had anticipated, but then, she reproved herself, she always was a lazy girl. She should have been preparing, not entertaining gentleman callers.

'Contaminate? I don't understand....'

Hester made a sound that could very possibly have been a snort, were she ever to do anything so unladylike. 'They aren't followers of Mr. Lokey, it seems. Or rather, their families aren't. It seems Mrs. Delaney tried to convert them and was received with a certain tolerance which turned rather swiftly to froideur when she made remarks about pagans and foreigners and how those not following Mr. Lokey would be - ahem - cursed.'

'Cursed! Surely she didn't actually say *cursed*?'

Hester smoothed the apron again, very firmly. 'It seems she did. Repeatedly. She also said that her son was not to mix with un-believers lest his spirit was dirtied by their false doctrines. I am very surprised she knew what any of that meant, but Tiffany is not a silly girl and she was quite serious when she repeated the conver-sation. She was of the opinion Mrs. Delaney had *learned it out of a book*, as she put it. She also felt Mrs. Delaney looked like *a proper Zombie*, apparently.'

'And Joey, did Tiff say anything...?'

'Confined to his bedroom it seems. Also, and I find this very telling, the Dave person has been shown the door as he apparently disagreed rather violently with Mrs. Delaney's new-found faith. Oh yes, and Mrs. Delaney takes Joey to commune with Mr. Lokey every night. Tiffany also said Joey threw a note down from his window to her - here it is, Tiffany allowed me to keep it.'

Lydia took the crumpled paper from Hester, noting how her friend's lips were pressed tight together, as pale and folded in as an early rose. She smoothed the scrap of lined paper and read the scrawled but forceful writing.

tiff tell the ladies it isnt my fault I cant come out no more I am sorry honest please help me its not right all this mums gone mad or somethin that lokey fella is well creepy I am scared tell the ladies theyll know what to do

'I am scared.' For Joey to admit he was scared was extremely worrying. Joey might be shaken, he might be worried, or nervous, but in normal circumstances nothing would have induced him to admit he was frightened. Girls were scared - well, not Tiff, who was frightened of nothing - but girls in general. Joey's manly pride would not allow fear to enter into his personal lexicon. And the part about 'the ladies' knowing what to do? What could we do? thought Lydia anxiously. Inform Social Services that a young boy had been taken by his concerned mother to prayer meetings and was forbidden to play in the street? That the same mother had learnt long words, thrown her bully of a boyfriend out and seemed intent on leading a religious life? Lydia could well imagine the patronising, dismissive tone on the end of the phone, edged with the kind of irritation and contempt reserved for 'hysterical old women' who saw plots and threats everywhere.

But as the friends sat on the creaking swing-seat shaded by the faded green canopy, while Dion sprawled by the side in the sun, listening intently as ever, and the scent of rosemary and moss-roses evaporated into the still, warm air, Lydia knew, in a way she could barely articulate, that something was dreadfully wrong.

'Lyddie, something is dreadfully wrong' said Hester, firmly.

Lydia jumped. 'Er, yes,' she replied. 'There is. Very wrong.'

What she didn't say was just how wrong she thought it actually was. That a child they knew and loved - yes, loved - was being exposed to such baleful influences worried her terribly. And she did love Joey. So did Hester, that was obvious. Of course all children were sacred and you shouldn't have favourites, it wasn't fair, but Joey was so, so *dear,* such an intelligent, comely lad, so full of life and - well, he was their boy. Their fosterling. And yes, thought Lydia sadly, they were after all, two childless women, with a great deal of maternal love to give. Would that it had been otherwise, but what was, was, as Gyremandel always said. *Don't fight the unchangeable, it is unproductive and exhausting. Instead, use the resources you have to achive what you may.* Indeed, thought Lydia, indeed.

'Hester, I'm going to see what's happening with Joey. If you don't want to be involved, I quite understand, I....'

Hester and Dion both looked at Lydia. Hester spoke - for both of them, had she but known it. 'I am with you, dear Lydia, all the way. Do you need anything to…?'

Lydia began to weave a complicated pattern in the air with her fingers, the flashing gems - balas rubies and diamonds - on her rosy, tapering fingers coruscating in the sunlight. 'No, Hester, I don't need anything.…'

The scent of patchouli and oud filled the air, and the buzzing of bees vibrated with increasing intensity as those glittering fingers danced. The air shimmered in opalescent purple shot with gold, and Hester and Dion watched fascinated as the garden seemed to recede around them. It was as if they were simultaneously both in Hester's garden and also in Joey's bedroom, in his house, down on the Terrace.

Joey sat on his bed, unaware of his invisible guests, on his Manchester United pattern quilt, gazing glumly at the wall where an empty wall-mounted TV shelf and a pristine white patch on the battered paintwork behind showed that a TV had recently been there. There were no books on his old desk - none of his adventure tales or Horrible History volumes - and no computer. Wires on the desk showed where the old PC had been removed. On the Manchester United mouse pad sat one, lone spiral-bound book: 'Ray's Children's Crusade - The Lokey Way For Kids'. The brightly-coloured cover showed Mr. Lokey, dressed in careful casuals, smiling down at a freckled pair of blond children, a boy and a girl, obviously siblings. 'Parental Advisory - Not Needed! Ray's Way Is The Right Way For Your Troubled Child! Trust In Ray - Pray With Ray!'

Lydia heard Hester gasp as she saw the book. But Joey heard nothing except the homely, familiar sounds from outside - a lawn mower stuttering, children playing, distant traffic noise, a fashionable pop song playing faintly on someone's stereo. The sun filtered in through the faded curtains and cast a glowing lozenge on the dirty carpet. Sighing, Joey lay back on his bed, and put his hands behind his head. Tears sparkled in his tired eyes. As he seemed about to fall asleep, the door was unlocked and Mrs. Delaney came in, carrying a worn plastic beaker of water. Joey opened his eyes, quickly wiped his face with his hand and sat up again, reaching for the water. Mrs. Delaney held it out of his reach, her expression stern. She was wearing a shapeless, calf-length blue smock dress, a bobbly white cardigan and flat brown sandals. Her bright false nails were gone and her dyed hair, now showing grey at the roots, was scraped back into a tight pony-tail with a plain rubber band. Not a scrap of make-up adorned the pallid face that once looked like it was carrying the entire cosmetic contents of Superdrug. She scowled fiercely at the boy, who hung his tousled head miserably.

'Well?' she demanded, putting the beaker on the desk roughly. 'Well? You gonna behave or am I gonna have to make you fast your-self pure another night? I saw you chuck something out the window at that unbeliever girl, I....'

Joey's voice was raw with misery. He picked at the quilt cover and gazed up at his mother, his face desolate. 'Mum, that's Tiff. She's not a - she's Tiff, you know her, she's my frien -'

Quick as an adder darting, Mrs. Delaney smacked the boy hard round the side of the head, knocking him backwards onto the bed. Lydia heard Dion start up and growl, and she gestured him to be still. Tears now poured in earnest from Joey's hazel eyes as first the white, then the red mark of his mother's hand blazed on his soft cheek and he huddled himself back against the wall.

'You see? You see what you made me do?' raged Mrs. Delaney. 'Oh, you're a devil and no mistake - you always was. And now! Carrying on with those dirty foreigners, those unbelievers, like they was real people! Polluted, you are. Filthy. Well, I've got news for you. Your father...'

Joey jumped up eagerly, his face full of hope. 'Dad! Is Dad coming? Oh...'

Mrs. Delaney smirked, and the hand that had hit her child now smoothed down the skirt of her dress. Her face filled with a power-ful, almost sensual pleasure. 'Your dad? Oh no - he's not coming.

Not now, not never. The dirty get got himself killed last night, in a car smash in Ireland. You'll not see your precious dad no more, so it's just you and me, Joseph, just you and me. You'd best get your head round cleansing that rebellious spirit, son, because until you do, you're staying in here fasting. Stop blubbing. That man never loved you, you was just a mistake to him. Just a nothing. It was all lies him saying he was coming for you. He never would have. Never. Oh, shut up - shut up! Right - you're in here 'til you get your mind right - and you won't be needing this, either.'

With that, Mrs. Delaney seized the beaker of water and swept out of the door, slamming it shut and locking it behind her.

On the bed, Joey lay weeping. The watchers heard his muffled sobs as Joey said '*Dad, oh dadda*' over and over. In the garden Hester clutched Lydia's arm, and Dion's hackles bristled and his tail was like a bottle-brush as a low growl issued from his throat.

Hester, distraught, whispered to Lydia. 'Lyddie, please, please do something.'

Lydia frowned in concentration and a heavy scent of lavender and honey, laced with something Hester recognised as poppy, hazed the rippling air with blue luminescence. As they watched, the boy seemed to relax, and his strained, white face smoothed out into the contours of peaceful sleep.

And the watchers were back in Hester's bee-filled, herb-scented garden.

Tears poured down Lydia's pale, exhausted face unashamedly. Hester dabbed at her own eyes with one of Mr. Marvell's hankies and her expression was indescribable - but it was a blessing for Mrs. Delaney she was not within her reach at that moment. Hester looked across at Lydia and, alarmed at her appearance, jumped up and raced into the house for a restorative, and to put the kettle on. Lydia lay back on the swing seat cushions, feeling as if all her strength had drained away into the ground. The air suddenly shifted and before her, incandescent in his rage, stood the human form of Dionysus.

His eyes blazed ferociously, still the topaz, slit pupil eyes of his cat form. 'My queen, this is beyond bearing. The woman must die - she will destroy your fosterling, she is a base and vile creature in bondage to a false creed, let me - '

Lydia gestured weakly, yet with a power that stopped Dion, panting, as he spoke. 'No, my lord, no. In this age such things are not permitted.'

'Yet it is permitted to torment a mere child? It is permitted to starve him and deny him water in the heat of the day? To taunt him with the death of his blood father?'

'Behind closed doors, in this age, humans such as these do as they choose. Children are merely possessions to the likes of them - to trade for favours, to exercise power over - pah! They don't consider how the children feel or what is created in their spirits by such things. Would that I could loose your fury, beloved, but I cannot, I cannot. We must find the deeper cause, the root of this, for it is not as simple as it might seem - but go, in your other guise, see if you can find a way to watch the boy, dearest one.'

Dion bowed and reaching out, took Lydia's hand and kissed it. She felt his hot breath on her chilled flesh. 'Your wish, my queen, is ever my command.'

And he was gone, just as Hester returned with the tea tray and a nostrum fizzing in a small blue glass bottle. She paused, puzzled, on the top step into the garden for a second then carried on, shaking her head.

'I rather fear this is all getting to me somewhat - really - I could have sworn - no, it's too silly - but I thought I saw a *naked man* wearing nothing but a sort of leafy garland in his hair standing over you, Lyddie. The worst of it is, he looked so *familiar* - I - well. Here, drink this Lydia, yes, all of it - and here's some tea. Oh, Lydia, are you all right? I have never seen such a scrying, never. Not even Mr. Marvell could have done it - it was as if we were actually there, there in that room with poor Joey and that *dreadful* woman. I feel I'm italicising but honestly, I am quite beside myself with crossness, I feel so frustrated - we must *do* something Lyddie. It's just - just horrible.'

Lydia sighed and obediently drank the potion, which tasted of elderflower and faintly, of something earthier and more unusual. She felt the tendrils of its healing power unfurl through her system and, closing her eyes, took a moment to allow it to work fully. Breathing slowly to calm herself, she opened her eyes again.

The garden seemed to her to be quite exquisite. The green of the herb plot - varying from the greyish mauve velvet of sage through to the sizzling aromatics of rosemary, the flirtatious ruffle of parsley and tender basil - was glorious and seemed to settle her gently back into herself. The heavy-headed old roses, blush-pink, yellow and purple-red, vaporising the vanilla and citrus of their heady aromas into the warm air, were intoxicating. Life, in fact the physical world, was good. It was.

She took Hester's cold hand in her warm one. 'Yes, it's dreadful. I agree. We will - we must - do something to help that child. I know people would say it's none of our business, that the boy has a roof over his head, he's not being beaten, he's not - in general - being starved. He goes to school. He is being taught a moral code…'

'But Lydia - really - what we saw was…'

Lydia smiled at her friend's righteous indignation. It was a sad smile - tender and full of love. She patted Hester's hand. 'What would you say, my dear, to the official you tried to speak with about this? That you'd seen inside the child's house in a vision? That esoteric practices had allowed you to witness his mother torturing him? May I be frank? They'd lock you up, and me too.'

Hester turned her head away, gazing apparently intently at the geraniums in the lichen-embroidered terracotta planter by the back door. Had a person looked closely, they might have seen the crystal glitter of extra moisture in her grey eyes - but then, the sun was bright and it can make you blink and have to rub your eyes. Just as

Hester had to do before turning back, with a determined expression, to her friend.

'I quite understand. What do you suggest?'

Lydia put down her tea-cup. 'A visit to Mr. Ray Lokey. I feel the need for spiritual guidance, don't you, my dear?'

Chapter Ten

The Bountiful Haven Life Church was a huge, undistinguished warehouse-style building painted in a pale grey that served to point up the enormous cobalt blue and orange backlit plastic sign over the front doors: 'The Bountiful Haven Life Church - A Place Of Peace'. Smaller lettering indicated the sign itself was a gift from Lassiter's Signs Ltd, Competitive Prices - Great Quality! The doors themselves were vast, glittering sheets of plate glass, standing open as a steady stream of people climbed the broad flight of stone steps and entered their cavernous maw.

Hester paused on the steps. The two women had, without conferring, each decided to put their nicest clothes on. To dress up a little, in fact. Neither could have explained this impulse but individually they both felt somehow armoured in their good clothes. They lent a formality to their excursion. Hester was attired in her best black frock with her Mizpah brooch, and carried a large black finely crocheted lacy stole of her own manufacture over her arm, alongside an enormous black leather bag containing, Lydia knew, everything Hester might ever want or need for a six month sea voyage or similar. She smelt of lavender from her own garden and looked like the perfect widow, which of course, she was. She also, unusually, looked somewhat nervous. Lydia - smelling deliciously of a perfume called Amber Precieuse - had chosen a very plain ankle-skimming vintage Calvin Klein dress of a subdued shade of dusky rose pink with only very small diamond studs in her ears (blue-white, half-carat, flawless, set in platinum, nothing showy), and a deep pink pashmina shawl over the arm holding a tiny light tan bag that toned with her pretty sandals. They both looked extremely respectable.

Hester cleared her throat. 'Lyddie - I must say I feel unaccountably uncomfortable. I have attended dozens of services of many denominations quite happily - but this…'

She gestured with her unencumbered arm at the squat building. 'Lyddie, what faith is this church? I don't see anything to indicate what doctrine they follow, just nebulous statements about peace. And apparently, the cheapness of their signage.'

Lydia stepped down to Hester and smiled reassuringly. 'I'm not sure myself. I have tried to look deeper but they're protected by a number of quite efficient Glamours and a definite Block. I assume they're Christian - yet, is that what we're supposed to assume? I agree, there's nothing saying they are, yet the - Hester, I just don't know. It is strange, but I feel we simply must go and investigate, even though I agree with you, it's very unsettling.'

Hester sighed. 'I just saw the editor of the E&C - Mr. Marvell once had dealings with him. A very ignorant person. Very well, yes, we must find out what we can. After all, if the great and the good are attending, who are we, mere citizens, to demur.'

The hall was decorated throughout in the Haven's signature blue and orange and managed to look like a cross between a corporate hotel lobby and a high-class mortuary chapel. Massive orange pleated velour drapes framed the high stage which was flanked by colossal imitation flower arrangements balancing precariously on white pillars. The ceiling was punctuated by vast crystal chandeliers and the plush blue nylon carpets muffled the murmuring of the assembled congregation. The air hummed with a cloying peach-scented air freshener and was so conditioned as to be faintly chilly. The lights were low, but not so low as to encourage distraction or a lack of focus on the great screen behind the stage on which was projected a silent film of abstract colours flowing and blending together whilst words like 'peace', 'faith', 'love' and 'charity' appeared and dissipated across the mesmeric patterns; it was like an enormous screensaver, fascinating yet soporific. Lydia could not help but think it must all have cost a great deal of money. *A very great deal of money*, she thought, noticing the state of the art sound system, something she knew about through a previous amour during the heady days of the Eighties. *Oh Bruce*, she thought nostalgically, *what would you make of this gig? Hardly your scene. Far too corporate for you. How strange it is, and how very strange nobody but my dear Hester and I seem to find it strange.*

Hester and Lydia seated themselves at the back, by the aisle. Next to them sat an earnest-looking bespectacled young blonde woman with her hair tightly braided into two plaits. Further along were a family with three little children all of whom were very quiet, and dressed, as the young woman was, in an extremely conservative way, with clothes that looked almost deliberately shabby and threadbare. There was something almost theatrical in their appearance, and that of the majority of the audience, as if they were playing the part of what they thought a poor person should look like. They had an air of wearing almost a kind of uniform - one that loudly proclaimed their disinterest in, and disdain of, material or worldly things.

They all gazed unblinkingly at the screen. The words 'brother-hood' and 'decency' bloomed then faded on a shimmering aqua background that turned to a luminous purple. Up and down the aisles, slim, handsome young men in grey lounge suits and white shirts with blue bow-ties handed out leaflets and received envelopes from the crowd. *It must be a collection*, thought Lydia - *and some of those envelopes look rather thick.* The young woman next to her clutched such an envelope tightly in her hands, and Lydia noticed she, and a number of the other women, such as the mother further along, were wearing identical broad silver rings with an inscription on them. Without seeming to stare, she read the girl's ring. It said 'purity' in an Old English script. And there was a symbol after it. Lydia knew the symbol. It was the rune Algiz. Reversed. It meant consumption by divine forces. A very unpleasant concept. She began to suspect quite strongly this all might be a lot worse than she had at first thought.

The girl next to her turned to face her, her eyes shining. 'Yes, the Lord is coming. You must be patient, sister. Are you and your friend newbies?'

Her accent and demeanour spoke of what was usually described as a 'decent upbringing' and her face, devoid of cosmetics, was rosy and shining from being thoroughly scrubbed.

Hester and Lydia looked at each other. Lydia smiled at the girl and a scent of fresh roses and benzoin cut briefly but intoxicatingly through the synthetic peach. 'Newbies? I'm sorry, I...'

'Oh,' cried the girl, twisting the silver ring on her finger, 'I mean, you're new to our family. You've not been before, I haven't noticed you and you do look singular. I mean, nicely, but - we, *we* don't dress to impress, as our Lord says...'

Hester craned round Lydia. 'Your Lord?'

The girl blushed furiously. 'I - well, that's what the family call Ray, we call him our Lord, you know, because he's shown us the Light. You'll see, once he speaks - oh, it's marvellous, really, and...'

'Shhh, please, sister, you're disturbing our vibrations' the young mother said in a strong midlands accent, as she put her hand, her silver band glinting in the hazy light, on the girl's arm, restraining her. The girl blushed even more and mumbled an apology, then returned to gazing determinedly at the glowing screen.

Hester gave Lydia what is known as an old fashioned look. 'This is very odd,' she whispered in Lydia's ear. 'Are we in America? I can't believe all this nonsense, it's quite vulgar if you ask me and - '

'Shh,' whispered back Lydia, 'you're disturbing my vibrations.'

'Oh, very amusing,' grumbled Hester. 'Look - I do believe the show is starting.'

As Hester spoke, the young be-suited men darted back to the stage and lined up either side of it like an honour-guard. Their youthful faces were solemn, but spoke of a suppressed excitement, just as Lydia and Hester's neighbours' did. An almost palpable quiver ran through the auditorium as the music changed to something that sounded almost like Gospel, and a group of young people, of both genders, trooped onstage and arranged themselves in a semi-circle at the back. They were dressed in billowing, satiny blue robes with wide, white collars - choirboy style - and their faces also bore the look of barely-controlled excitement but mixed with the desire to giggle and shriek, as at a pop-star or celebrity. They cast sidelong glances at each other, and subtle jostling betrayed their anticipation.

The hall lights lowered, to a mass gasp. The girl next to Lydia and Hester squeaked excitedly. A wave of restlessness passed through the crowd, it was almost infectious. Lydia could feel the power of it, hysterical and volatile. The Gospel-type music swelled and rose, then a disembodied baritone American voice boomed from the speakers.

'Are you ready? Are you ready? Are you ready to *change your lives*?' it cried.

As one, the audience responded, 'Yes!'

The Voice seemed to chuckle paternally. 'I said, *are you ready to change your lives*?'

'YES!' came the screamed response. Lydia felt Hester grasp her hand.

'If you're ready, if you're ready - if you're truly, truly ready…' the Voice declaimed.

'WE ARE, WE ARE!' howled the audience while the honour-guard beamed and the blue-robed acolytes, eyes bright with fervour, raised their arms and chanted 'Change! Change!'

'Please welcome into your hearts….' The music lowered to an anticipatory hum, 'welcome the man who's come to save you, the man who loves you one and all, the man *you have been* wait-*ing* for - RAAAAAAYYYY LOKKKKEY!'

The drums rolled, the crowd erupted in screams and shouts, girls rushed the stage only to be caught and returned, half-fainting, by the honour-guard. It was like some strange pop music concert, thought Hester, with Ray Lokey in place of The Beatles. The choir swayed in unison, eyes half-closed, and chanted 'Ray, Ray, Ray, Ray, Ray...'

'My God' whispered Hester, appalled, her eyes riveted to the chaotic spectacle.

'No, not your god. Not anyone's god anymore, I think' returned Lydia with a steely note in her usually mellifluous voice.

The spotlight illuminated a central microphone in a halo of white-gold and on to the stage strode a tall, lean figure dressed in loose, worn jeans, scuffed tan boots and a blue plaid shirt buttoned to the neck and wrists. He seized the microphone as if it were the most precious thing in the world and gazed at the audience with ice-blue eyes gleaming with tears of love.

'I hear, you. I hear your call. I hear you my lost ones, I hear your pain - but do not fear. No, do not fear. I am with you, yes I am, I am with you, Ray is with you. Ray is here, Ray is here...'

And so it went on, the crowd ecstatic, the girl next to Lydia on her knees weeping, the little family standing punching the air, holding the baby aloft while the toddlers cried unnoticed. All seduced by the warm, passionate timbre of Ray Lokey's beautiful voice, a voice so loaded with commanding frequencies and thick with ancient Glamours that even Lydia had a little trouble resisting its terrible allure. She glanced, worried, at Hester.

Hester sat, her face utterly calm as the hall seethed and shrieked around her. Her grey eyes were cool and thoughtful, her brows level. The only indication she felt anything at all was the almost imperceptible bloom of faintest pink on her pale cheekbones. Hester, Lydia saw, was thinking.

The harangue continued unabated from the stage. Occasionally, an audience member would throw themselves forward screaming for Ray to forgive their sins, their wickedness, how they needed Ray to save them from themselves. They would be rewarded by a re-doubling of hysteria from the crowd, the firm restraint of the honour-guard and Ray, barely pausing in his flow, reaching down and touching their forehead with his long, white fingers. Then they'd faint ecstatically and have to be carried off by the honour-guard. The girl next to Lydia radiated envy every time this occurred. Lydia wondered why she didn't throw herself at the stage like the others to receive the touch and the attention. Perhaps she hadn't sinned deeply enough, Lydia mused. As if she could.

Slowly, Ray Lokey brought the hysteria down and began to stride around the stage as if deeply troubled. Again, Lydia noted his resemblance to the young Kirk Douglas, a very marked resemblance indeed. She whispered as much to Hester.

'Who?' whispered Hester in return.

'Kirk Douglas - the actor - you know, Gunfight At The OK Corral, The Vikings - you must remember The Vikings, it had Tony Curtis in it too, and - '

'Shh, Lydia, please, this is no time to reprise your curious taste in films...'

'I wasn't, I only remarked - ' But Lydia stopped mid-sentence, as Ray stopped pacing and returned to centre stage, his expression melancholic, a man with the burdens of a wicked world on his broad, athletic shoulders. The crowd fell silent, except for a few scattered sobs. The stage lights became softer. The choir hummed.

'You know, people, you know how I strive to bring the young ones into the light.' His tone was sorrowful. The girl in the next seat wept into a tissue. The crowd murmured '*We know, Lord, we know.*'

'You call me Lord - yes, I hear you, you call me, a worthless man, Lord...' Ray turned his handsome face into the spotlight and tears ran down his cheeks, a lot of tears. The crowd cried, '*No, no, not worthless...*' as if on cue.

Ray sighed and shook his head. 'Well, I wish I was. I wish I was that strong, but I ain't strong, folks, I ain't strong, for I have wrestled this past week with a young 'un gripped in the claws of the Evil One, bound tight to that wicked force, cleaving unto its darkness like a child at the breast. And will this child repent of his ways and stop breakin' his poor, lovin' mother's heart? No - no he will not! He will not! People, it's gonna take all your prayers, all your prayers to bring this baby back home, yes it is! Yes it is! Help me save him! Help me save him! Bring him to me here - yes, bring him here so these good people can save him with their prayers!'

And to Lydia and Hester's absolute horror, a member of the suited battalion dragged a struggling Joey onto the stage, followed by a black-clad Mrs. Delaney, clutching a hankie, her face a mask of pious grief.

Hester half-rose. 'Joey - oh, no, no, Joey....' Lydia had never heard such passion in her friend's voice before. She herself was trembling with anger, her hands visibly shaking.

'I'm praying, I'm praying for the wicked little sinner, Ray, I'm...' shouted the girl.

'Shut up!' hissed Lydia with such force and with such modulations in her voice, the girl dropped back into her seat, silent, her eyes wide and shocked behind the greasy lenses of her glasses.

Horrified, the friends watched as Ray put his hand on Joey's bowed head, nodding sympathetically at Mrs. Delaney, who stifled sobs with her hankie and leant - a trifle more than was necessary - on the muscular arm of the handsome young black man who had brought them in. His face was impassive.

'Boy' intoned Ray, 'look at me. Look at me. I'm your friend, I'm your pal, you gotta just trust me - see, I'm a grown-up, and grown-ups know what's best for kids, yes, we do. I know you think you know what's best, I know the television and the films and those rap records tell you us grown-ups are old has-beens...' Ray paused to give a rueful grin. 'I know they say, why, we don't know what it's like to live in the modern world, and you listen to that, don't you? You listen to the Evil One's voice through your Playstation and your X-Box, your horror films and your TV pro-*grammes*. But no more, no more of that, Joey Delaney. You belong to us now, you're in our family - isn't that right, folks?'

And the hall erupted. Mrs. Delaney wept. The choir shouted, *'Ray! Ray!'* and Ray Lokey, unobserved except by two middle-aged ladies sitting at the back of the auditorium, made a swift, complex pattern in the air above Joey's head with his long, bony fingers.

'The Adamantine Concurrence' said Hester, grimly. 'The utter fiend.'

Swiftly, Lydia grabbed Hester's huge bag and thrust it between herself and the praying girl beside her, forming an impromptu shield. Then, eyes closed in concentration, she wove a deft and complex Glamour. The air suffused with the arcane odour of mandrake, and a shimmer of deep violet shot with emerald hazed the air for a second. The girl noticed nothing, nor did the family further along - except for one of their children, a girl of about five, who stared fascinated as the glimmering mist evaporated.

On the stage, as Lydia's counter-Glamour negated Ray's device, Joey's head came up and he stared wildly into the crowd as Ray gripped his thin shoulder.

Hester stood up. Straight as a spear, her dark brows pulled level over her blazing grey eyes, she raised her hand, palm outwards like an archaic statue. A kind of cool fury radiated from her and the expression on her white face - well, Lydia hoped it would never be directed at herself.

Joey saw Hester and shouted, twisting out of Ray's hold. He ducked past his mother who flailed wildly at him and evaded the guard who had brought him onstage, running and scrambling into the wings and out of the ladies' sight.

Chaos erupted as the crowd rose to its feet screaming and gabbling as if Satan himself had strolled into their midst - the noise was terrific and Hester sat back down rather quickly. The girl next to Lydia swooned, her eyes rolling back and her flat chest rising and falling rapidly as she muttered incoherently. The young mother, shaking with emotion, helped her to her seat again and - ignoring her children's frightened cries - prayed frantically with the girl for the 'wicked boy' who had been 'possessed' before their very eyes.

On the stage, as the choir hugged each other and wept behind him, Ray Lokey's cold, piercing eyes swept the hall, seeking those who had interfered with his plans. He stopped, and a strange judder passed through him, like a horse's skin when a fly lands on it. He glared into the pandemonium.

Hester gripped Lydia's hand and whispered, 'Lyddie - he's seen us - that creature - he knows we're here.'

Lydia gathered her bag and shawl. 'Quickly - let's go - let's find Joey.'

The friends got up and, as unobtrusively as possible, left the auditorium. Behind them they could hear Ray's unctuous tones begging his audience to pray with him for the demon child who had shown the dreadful power of the Evil One to everyone present. Lydia and Hester hurried into the vestibule and towards the great glass doors. Somewhere, out there, away from all this dreadful nonsense, Joey needed help. They almost ran towards the entrance, Lydia's pashmina fluttering behind her like a pennant.

A tall, be-suited figure blocked their path.

'Excuse me, ladies. Mr. Lokey would like to speak with you, if it's convenient.'

It was the honour guard who had brought Joey up onto the stage. His beautiful ebony face was expressionless, his voice deep, melodious, and warm. His wide shoulders and height were an effective barrier.

'No, young man, it is not convenient,' Hester said sharply. Lydia scrutinised the looming figure carefully and then nudged Hester quite sharply with her elbow.

'As my friend says, it is not convenient, but we are prepared to give Mr. Lokey a few moments. I trust he will not detain us long?'

The guard bowed slightly. 'Of course not, madam. He merely wants a few moments of your time in private.'

Hester gave Lydia one of her looks, but held her tongue. Lyddie was up to something, she could tell. But what?

'Please,' said the huge guard, 'follow me.'

Chapter Eleven

As the friends accompanied the guard through windowless blue-carpeted corridors then up a short flight of stairs, the stale air leavened with more of the peach air freshener and a faint odour of synthetic fabrics and carpets made their journey seem as if they were on some kind of awful cross-channel ferry. As they got closer towards their interview with Ray Lokey, Hester felt herself somewhat puzzled by the young man they followed. They passed innumerable faux-stained-glass 'Art' hangings, and printed canvasses depicting doves, rainbows, buxom winged blonde women in white nighties and big-eyed children clutching each other, and Hester had the distinct, but very strange impression that she was walking behind not one, but two people. As if one person overlaid the other. She glanced at Lydia, who walked purposefully, her rosy lips compressed and pale, her expression calm. If only she could share her thoughts with Lyddie, if only she could....

Lydia slipped her arm through Hester's. 'You're right, my dear, all is not what it seems. Be alert.'

Hester gave Lyddie's arm a squeeze. It really was amazing how they felt the same feelings sometimes. Comforted, but still puzzled, she held her head up high and assumed a regal look. *Never let them see you're afraid* had been one of dear Mr. Marvell's maxims. She had never needed that sage advice more, she thought.

'Please wait here a moment, ladies. I will apprise Mr. Lokey of your presence' said the guard, indicating some chairs placed in the corridor next to the door to an office. The metal nameplate read 'Ray Lokey - Private' in black on gold. Lydia inclined her head and sat. Hester, ablaze with curiosity, chose to stand.

'Apprise Mr. Lokey of our presence?' murmured Hester. 'Really, how archaic. Or indeed, American. They have that excesssive formality of speech - oh, Lydia, I am rather nervous, though I hate to admit it.'

Lydia squeezed her friend's arm again comfortingly. 'Me too, dear. But think of Joey. And for that matter, all the other Joeys - because I fully imagine this is not the first child Ray Lokey has influenced. Nor will he be the last - unless…'

'Unless? Lydia, what are you going to do?'

Lydia turned her lovely, flower-like face to Hester, her faintly tanned goldenness flushed with a hint of wild rose, her wide blue eyes sparkling with an intensity rare in such an easy-going - *nay, hedonistic*, thought Hester - character. The charming, curvaceous blonde with a dancing smile and adorable dimples who seemed so youthful despite her middle years, was replaced by a woman of regal and commanding aspect. *Queenly*, thought Hester, *she is positively queenly*. And she drew herself up even more upright beside the orange velour upholstered chairs, taking her cue from Lydia. This was no time for weakness. She must remember the child - the children.

The tall guard reappeared. 'Mr. Lokey will see you now.'

'I bet he will,' said Lydia, sotto voce.

Hester permitted herself a slight smile. She could not imagine a mere wandering preacher could stand up to Lydia in this mood - he'd better beware.

The office the friends were shown into was huge - the undistin-guished laminate door opened onto a very large, spacious penthouse room with beautiful floor-to-ceiling windows giving a stunning view of the town and the countryside beyond. The décor was modern Scandinavian - but of the artisan, rather than IKEA sort. Hand-woven beige drapes embroidered on the hems with red folkloric patterns framed the great window and swept the pine floor which was scattered with tousled cream wool and reindeer skin rugs. A long, curved sofa upholstered in more of the handwoven beige fabric and studded with similarly embroidered cushions sat opposite the window, and a low abstract pine coffee table in front of it held a beaten pewter carafe and goblets on a matching tray. Huge framed paintings of snowy mountainous landscapes - heavy with impasto - hung on the cream walls. It was like an advert for holidays in Norway.

At another abstract pine piece, this time a huge desk supported on massive rough cast glass legs, leaning back in an ergonomic beige leather office chair, his long, bony fingers steepled in front of his fox-face, sat Mr. Ray Lokey, radiating the unctuous confident smoothness of a used car salesman and chuckling benignly. The huge guard stood behind him, staring at a point in the middle distance. Two matching chairs with high carved backs stood in front of the desk - Ray motioned grandly for the friends to sit.

'Welcome! Welcome to my house! Please, be seated. Now, may I offer you ladies some refreshment? I have an excellent coffee - or some Earl Grey? Or perhaps some cool Lingonberry juice? It's quite delicious.'

Gone was the rough-edged, ingenuously sincere man of the people. Close to, the working man's checked shirt was a beautiful cotton and silk material exquisitely cut and hand-stitched, the jeans patently Armani. And Ray himself was barbered and coiffured to perfection, his jaw smooth and pink, his thick, shining rufous hair swept back from a romantic widow's peak. His hands were very clean and the flat, rather over-long, nails buffed to a fine polish. He looked - expensive. Powerful. Hester pulled herself even straighter in the uncomfortable artistic chair.

'No, thank you, Mr. Lokey. We don't require refreshment.' Lydia's voice was cool and firm, her demeanour one of a woman of substance bestowing a favour on a tiresome underling. A flash of annoyance passed over Ray's face, quickly replaced with a broad smile. He motioned to the guard who silently left the room through another door.

'Well, I'm definitely going for the Lingonberry juice, it's my favourite. Let me know if you change your mind.'

'We won't. And let's get to the point, Mr. Lokey. You must release the boy Joey Delaney.' Lydia leant forward slightly. 'He is not yours, nor will he ever be. None of these children are. Your time is past, you must go to the place awaiting you. Your time here is long over.'

Swiftly, anger distorted Ray's face. Hester gasped involuntarily at the cold savagery in his pale, arctic eyes. He swept his hand through his hair and snarled at Lydia, his voice thick with modulations Hester had only guessed were possible and now wished heartily she had never heard. Ancient frequencies laced his speech, the homely English distorted by a warped twist that rendered the words almost unbearable. Hester shuddered and even Lydia paled - they could hardly have described how Ray Lokey's tone made them feel - it was the psychic equivalent of nails being dragged slowly down a blackboard. It was vile. The dying sun outside the shining windows darkened with cloud, and a sudden sharp breeze whipped through the young saplings planted around the building. An odour of burning peat, copper and decay filled the air. Lydia - though trembling slightly - did not flinch.

'You cannot order me to do anything! You say my time is past - what of yours, old queen? Your people are long fled, why do you tarry? And this one - pah! She does not even know who she - '

'Be still.' Lydia's voice was commanding, imperious. To Hester's astonished eyes she seemed to glow with a shimmering light. 'I am not alone here, my lord is with me, and I have lived here longer than you. I do not need the Essence anymore, as you apparently do. I do not batten on their frail hopes or their undefended young.'

'Oh,' sneered Lokey furiously, sitting back in his chair, 'you're not alone? You call that degenerate beast who guards you a companion? Oh yes, I can sense him, his scent is all over you. Whatever he once was, my dear, he is no longer. Your people were ever effete and spineless. He is of no interest to me, I am not frightened of such as he. My folk were always strong, brave, unflinching - we *deserved* the people's respect. We have it still - did you not witness that this evening? Where are *your* devotees?'

'Excuse me' said Hester, suddenly, in her best librarian voice, usually reserved for litter-louts and drunks. 'Forgive me, Lydia, but can someone please explain to me what all this has to do with your extraordinary and inappropriate behaviour towards Joey Delaney, Mr. Lokey.' Hester sat back, clutching her enormous black handbag to her maidenly bosom.

Outside, the lowering clouds shifted, and a palmate ray of light broke through. Lydia and Ray Lokey, interrupted, gazed at Hester in astonishment. At the same time, the guard returned with Ray's juice, in a blue glass tumbler. He took a sip and seemed to recover himself.

'Thank you, Andvari' he said, pulling at the collar of his shirt. The guard said nothing.

Lydia smiled coolly. 'Andvari? He's forgiven you then, for robbing him of his golden hoard? Is that how you afforded all this? You're in partnership now? Greetings, old one. I thought I recognised you. Hester, please meet Andvari the Dwarf, a shape-shifter more used to water than land. Congratulations on a very pleasing aspect, Andvari - though you must be missing your tarn in this dry place.'

Hester felt herself gaping and swiftly pulled herself together. The guard bowed slightly. 'Indeed, my lady,' he murmured sonorously, and for a disorientating and impossible split second, Hester saw in the same space occupied by the tall, handsome black youth, a gnarled, powerful, dark-visaged creature with weedy strands of greenish hair framing a warty, hideous face studded with a pair of glittering, glaucous eyes, and skin sheened with fish scales. He smiled at her, his snaggle-toothed mouth a cavern of peat-water and cold depths. She shuddered and instinctively made a warding sign. The dwarf-image vanished and the guard swayed slightly where he stood.

Lokey turned his attention to Hester like a striking falcon.

'Oh, none of that please, Andvari is very sensitive. I wouldn't want to reciprocate.'

Hester, though thoroughly unnerved, presented her usual imperturbable front. She would not let this - this - whatever he was - know that she, the Widow Marvell, was scared. She was an historian and a scientist. She was an Englishwoman.

'Please don't threaten me. You cannot hurt me. I am interested only in the whereabouts of Joey Delaney and insist you cease your activities regarding him, and indeed, any other children you may have influence over. What's more, Mr. Lokey, I think it would be a very good thing if you left our town forthwith.'

She sat back, her handbag firmly on her knee like a shield, her shining cap of silver hair a battle-helmet, her love of Joey a spear in her white hand.

Lydia was so proud of her she could hardly refrain from kissing her cheek. But that would never do, not at present. They had work to do.

Again, Ray steepled his fingers, the resemblance to Kirk Douglas pronounced. Hester now wondered what really occupied that lithe body. She felt a little dizzy as things she had only read about before happened in front of her very eyes. Shapeshifters? Evil Magic? Dwarves? Well, obviously she had often seen normal persons of restricted growth, or Little People as some preferred to call themselves, but not actual mythological Dwarves. Not ancient, water-spirit Dwarves masquerading as impossibly handsome black youths, anyway. It was as if her musty old books were suddenly being enacted in reality, before her very eyes.

Ray addressed Lydia. 'So, you keep her in ignorance of herself, eh? Why? Is she now your servant, she who bowed to no-one? I knew one such, our thunder-hammer, he imagined himself an athlete, a wrestler in the New World, posturing for all to see on the television. I sent him to his reward, still unaware of who he was.

What will you do with her? We cannot all live amongst the slaves, it would never do.'

'Joey Delaney.' Lydia's voice was a masterpiece of control. Hester, still puzzling over Ray's remark, barely heard. Ignorance of herself? She knew exactly who she - of course she did - she was Hester Marvell, widow of - she was - she was…. A veil seemed to drop from her grey eyes, and she felt herself almost split in two like the Dwarf Andvari; she saw the world and yet - another world was all around her…

The sun, hard yellow gold shining on the white portico, was almost too harsh to bear at midday even though it was still only May. The air was full of the scent of wild thyme, its precious oils evaporating in the heat. Bees buzzed lazily through the shrubs planted round the shrine. The sound of the maidens chanting echoed distantly and a slight, precious breeze stirred the long, white silk curtains bringing a faint hint of the sea. She stirred on her couch, sleepily watching the light glint off the gold trim on the snakeskin breastplate her father had given her and her favourite old bronze greaves propped against the whitewashed wall. It was robing day, the priestess was even now preparing the sanctuary. Her helmet and shield lay by the olive-wood table that bore a plate of apples and a dewy silver flacon of finest Chian cooled in a bowl of snow from - from Olympus - from Olympus - why - oh - oh - Olympus - Lydia - Dion - I am Hester Marvell, I am Hester ….

I am Athene.

I am Athene Parthenos and the Widow Hester Marvell. I am one and both. I am free again at last. The knowledge, strange yet comfortingly familiar, swept through her like a great wave from that dark sea; like an amnesiac waking to find the memories of her life returned safely to her, Hester was filled with joy. It seemed to her that she had known all along she was not as the world saw her and that this recovery of her true self was a liberation; as a butterfly emerges from the roiling confines of a chrysalis, shaking its glorious wings out to dry in the warmth of the sun, so Hester had been the chrysalis Athene had rested in until she was needed again. The recent past - who knew how many centuries - dropped away in concertinaed folds and Athene-Hester stepped from them gratefully. Time, after all, she mused, really was just a mode of thought.

Oh, Lydia - I know, I remember - not all, but enough, enough - I know who you are, I know why I knew you straight away, why I knew Dion, who Ray Lokey really is - I - I...

I must act. The child needs me. I was created to dispense justice, to protect such as he. I am the warrior-maid.

Hester coughed. 'Excuse me, Mr. Lokey. I know full well who I am, and who you are. I am also pleased to remain in this form unless you continue to refuse to return to me my ward, the human boy, Joey Delaney.'

Lydia's jaw dropped and she quickly scrambled to recover composure. Hester *knew*? For how long? Oh my, they were going to have an interesting night's talk after this battle was fought. She managed an expression of slight contempt for Lokey's ignorance. The air filled with the scent of cypress and the faint sound of bees.

'Unlike you, Mr. Lokey, we are not all bent on living in the past and re-creating old glories. Some of us are content to live quietly in this modern age. Now, the child?'

If Ray Lokey had been angry before, it was as nothing to the fury that surged through him and the entire room now. It was like a polar blast from savage arctic regions where nothing lived and every breath drawn crystallised into ice in lungs and heart. Ice crackled in the room, stiffening the curtains and forming icicles on the desk and light-fittings, turning them into glittering chandeliers. A roaring wind swept round the friends, real yet unreal, the sound and fury were there but no breath stirred their clothing or disturbed their hair. In the eye of Ray Lokey's hurricane Hester and Lydia sat untouched.

He was livid. Lydia could see plain as day that Ray was not used to anyone standing up to him. The maelstrom that he expelled was curiously childish, like a toddler having a tantrum - but on a massive scale and involving some pretty powerful elemental forces. Ray's face was ugly, blotched and distorted with the effort of his anger. Even

Andvari looked rather uncomfortable. It was like being at a dinner party where one guest completely loses their temper and everyone else has to sit there while they scream and shout, everyone embarrassed by the unwanted display and yet unable to leave out of politeness. Lydia sighed. Really, this was becoming boring. She made a gesture, the air stilled, and a refreshing aroma of orange-blossom and vanilla borne on a sparkling tangerine vapour floated ephemerally through the room. Andvari looked relieved, then cleared his throat and shifted from foot to foot. Lydia smiled at him and the dwarf-guard smiled back, then remembering where he was, quickly resumed his military stance.

Ray slumped in his chair, his expression sullen - not defeated, Hester noted, still dangerous, but, well, plain old sulky. Glancing at Lydia, who nodded, she spoke.

'Loki, mischief-maker, Norseman, trickster, shape-shifter, you must leave this place now, and release the human child. Return to the Cumbrian Stone that gave you your gate into this plane of existence, and never return...'

'Greek whore! I will not....'

'You will, Loki,' said Lydia firmly. 'Really, be reasonable. It's for your own good. I mean, how long do you think you can keep this up before all this dallying with humans and scrounging around for worship turns nasty? It always does, you know. We aren't meant to do that kind of thing anymore, this is a different age - come now, look what happened to Freya - what a disaster that was.'

Loki snorted. 'She was always a fool, always seeking attention, *Ooh, look at me! Aren't I pretty? Aren't I sexy?* - you goddesses of love are so spoilt. It's easy for you, all you have to do is bat your eyelashes, whip up a quick Glamour and everyone runs after you like idiots. *Real* gods, proper gods, struggle and work for what we earn, we deserve what we get, we *deserve* worship. Freya was weak, pathetic and weak, I tell you. As if being a film star was any substitute for genuine, authentic worship. She got what was coming to her. I have no sympathy with any of it so don't you try that tack on *me*, madam.'

Loki drummed his fingers on the desk and looked crossly out of the window, where a light rain had begun to fall, veiling the saplings and the road into Town in a silvery mist.

'You're sulking' said Lydia.

'I am not' muttered Loki.

'You are' interjected Andvari, calmly. 'You always do when you don't get your own way. Look what happened after all that Baldur stuff. You sulked for eons.'

'Sulked? Sulked? Who wouldn't after what they did to me?' snapped Loki. 'A silly accident and I get chained up for eternity with snakes - *snakes*, mind you, big ones - dripping venom in my face and only that silly bitch Sigyn to look after me. *Me* - who had hundreds of servants and slaves and concubines and...' He leered unbecomingly, '*shield-maidens*, I mean, shield-maidens, big sexy blonde ones. And suddenly I was a *nobody* stuck in some stinking cave with the wife. It was so *unfair*.'

Andvari rolled his broad shoulders and looked at the ceiling, now damp and dripping slightly. 'You did kill him. What were they supposed to do?'

'He provoked me! Oh, right, so it's OK to pick on the ginger god, is it? Yeah, let's all have a go at the ginner? Let me tell you - you *dwarf*, you don't know how I suffered, how I....'

Lydia coughed discreetly. 'Loki, please. This is all very well but we must return to the matter in hand. The child, Joey Delaney...'

'Is mine by gift' Loki sneered savagely. 'His mother gave him to me of her own free will, in exchange for youth and beauty, the usual thing. Andvari dealt with it all. I have it in writing, signed in her own blood, which I am happy to make available for DNA testing. Andvari - get the contract. Sorry ladies, that brat is *mine*.'

Loki sat back, arms folded, looking smug. Hester resisted smacking his face, and instead gazed out at the perfectly normal, English town that was settling down for the night beyond the plate glass windows of Loki's eyrie. She sighed. What could these poor humans know of the colossal forces that flowed unseen, undreamed of, around them as they went about their daily lives. Such brief, brief lives, dominated by longings they barely understood and shaped by pressures and desires fed to them by predators who only wanted their money. Youth and beauty, indeed. To sell your child for such ephemera - to be persuaded by a handsome face flirting with you that your own son was worth nothing more than a quick Glamour and - A thought sprang on her like an arrow loosed from a tight-strung bow.

'You say Andvari dealt with this?' Hester demanded sharply, as the dwarf returned with a rolled parchment in his shapely hand.

'What?' said Loki crossly. 'Yes, of course he did. I don't bother myself with the likes of that trollop, not that she thinks that of course, the silly mare, I daresay she thinks I just love her to bits. Wouldn't be doing my job right if she didn't. Now, the contract states....'

Hester permitted herself a slight smile, which Lydia noted with some trepidation.

'The contract is void' said Hester, calmly. Everyone stared at her. She waved her hand negligently. 'It was obtained under false pretences. Mrs. Delaney sold her son to a person she believed was a tall, handsome, *human man*, not - and I beg your pardon, Andvari - an ancient dwarf nature spirit. She cannot have possibly known, therefore, what she was actually doing and since she has no concept whatever of religion or faith, she is doubly ignorant of the true nature of her action. The contract is void.'

Hester sat back, and Lydia wondered if high-fiving was appropriate behaviour for a lady.

'Rubbish' snapped Loki. 'I've done this a thousand times. The mother gives up her blood-child for the usual nonsense, I get full access to the kid's youth energies, I use them as fuel for my power, then dump the husk to do - whatever they do afterwards...'

'Tramps' said Andvari coolly. 'They become all those tramps, drunks and addicts that scrounge around the streets. All grey and shrivelled, the life sucked out of them - literally. Their only solace the bottle or the needle. No understanding of what was done to them, that their parents flogged them off for looks, or money or just to get rid of them because they were bored of the responsibility. They're the unwanted, the unloved. The used-up.'

Loki stared at the Dwarf. 'And your point is what, exactly?'

Andvari shrugged. 'Well, you asked - sort of. You should know, anyway, you're always going on about them in your sermons, saying they should be locked away or exorcised and things because they're....' Andvari sketched quote marks in the air.... 'demon-possessed. But hey, they aren't, really, are they? *You* made them. Well, not all of them obviously. There are natural causes, and other gods like you out there - I mean, that Tengri's not exactly scrupulous, is he? But you have done your fair share, as it goes.'

Loki turned fully to view Andvari. 'You're full of yourself today - what's got into you? And I've told you before, don't mention Tengri to me, thank you, the charlatan. Mongolia? Who cares about *Mongolia*? He can have it as far as I'm concerned. Anyway, you've been happy enough to share in the power, get yourself a nice new shape, live it up on my payroll - don't you dare throw it in my face now.'

'You're tired of it, though, aren't you, Andvari Tarn Lord? Tired of humans and the modern world. All the greed and noise and stink - how you miss the cool silence of the tarn and the Old World. No-one bothering you, just you and your hoard and perhaps, a comely dwarf maiden....' Lydia gazed at him sympathetically.

Andvari smiled. 'Well, there was a lass, a Rowan Dwarf...'

Loki grimaced. 'Oh please - spare me the sorry romances of the Elder Days - the boy is *mine*.'

Lydia, Hester and Andvari stared at Loki silently. Clouds of ice vapour started forming behind him as he brooded. Lydia wasn't sure but she thought she could see faint crow's feet forming by his beautiful eyes - did he need youth energy so badly? She didn't, never had - but she knew plenty who did, it was the richest, most pure energy going. Every time she opened a magazine it was packed with advice about how to simulate the essence of youth, as if face creams and paints could buy you what Loki and his ilk took directly from the spirits of the poor, unfortunate youngsters that came their way. She could always spot the rogue goddesses in the celebrity magazines, those unnaturally youthful faces with just a hint of incredible age in the eyes - singers, actresses - all craving the love and worship they'd had in former days. Now they gave huge concerts, or made blockbuster films, and jetted around the world being photographed, with handsome young men like Andvari's current incarnation carrying their handbags. They looked powerful and assured - but Lydia knew. Hathor and Ishtar for example - both of them world famous but as celebrities now, not deities. Dreadful cows the pair of them - literally in Hathor's case, thought Lydia. Oh, I shouldn't be so bitchy, but there you are - I can't help it, it's the truth. Grasping, avaricious, desperate old vamps doing anything to keep that worship, desperate to be young. Or at least, seem young. Maybe in the modern world the two were the same. And look at Loki. Despite all the blather about manly gods, he's no better than the girls.

Hester nudged her out of her reverie. 'Loki, you cannot deny your contract with the Delaney woman is void. Be logical, give up this boy, do not make me fight for him. Because I will, as will Aphrodite and Dionysius. Can you withstand three Olympians? The damage to you and yours would be colossal. Do you not recall the Dasht-e Lut Incident?'

Lydia shot an enquiring look at Hester, as did Andvari.

Loki cleared his throat. 'Er - well yes, of course I do, but that was…'

Hester smiled. 'Then you will remember that the damage and destruction of the Ahriman Global Industries plant was so huge as to register in the Richter Scale, and Ahriman himself was extinguished, not just in this plane but at least a dozen others. Think what might happen here. I concede that was Zeus's doing, but three of us are more than equal to his power.'

'Don't you threaten me!' blustered Loki.

'I have no wish to' said Hester, coolly. 'But either you release the boy or we will do what we have to. Won't we, Lydia?'

'Certainly, Hester. Whatever it takes. Give us the boy and go to another plane of existence. Really, there's a lot to choose from, it's not like you'll starve.'

Loki rubbed the famous cleft chin. Then he drummed his long fingers on the desk thoughtfully. Andvari sighed and Loki shot him a withering look. 'Oh - all right then. But under protest, let me warn you. I won't forget this. I'll have to start all over again somewhere else - it's so tedious, I just had this lot going along nicely.' He grinned coldly, baring perfectly white teeth. 'Don't think I'll forget this - I'll get you, you meddling bitches. Somehow, somewhere...' He snapped his fingers. 'Andvari! Get the bloody kid, and sort out what we'll need afterwards. I want my things from the hotel and the stored energy, obviously, and...'

Andvari looked at Loki contemptuously. 'Get it yourself. No, I mean it. She's right. I'm fed up with all this. I should never have let you persuade me to do it in the first place - meddling with humans, it never works, they've got no - no substance. I don't see the point of 'em - apart from your precious energy I suppose. But even that's cheating, just plain greedy. You can get it the old way, if you're prepared to work hard. But not you, you idle git. Never done a day's work in your life, just wheedled and nagged and tricked. I'm off to my tarn. I'll get the child then that's it - pack your own bags.'

'Oh, well done, Andvari!' cried Lydia.

'You were right, ma'am. I was just stuck in this rut, running after *him*.' Andvari jerked his thumb contemptuously at Loki, who glared at him. 'What do they say? I need some me-time.'

Loki swore long and hard in Old Norse, then got up. 'Get the kid, then do what you like, you ingrate. I'm off. I am a *god*, you know, I certainly don't need help from a bloody *dwarf*. As for you two - I'll see you again, never fear. This isn't over, not by a long chalk.'

He turned to face the trio and the borrowed form of Kirk Douglas melted from the actuality that supported it. Hester gasped as the room seemed to fill with the huge, warped, oak-hard shape of the real Loki, his shock of ragged, elf-locked dark red hair stark against his long, white, archaic face, a face almost mask-like in its rigidity, a half-sneering, half-ingratiating expression carved into the ancient ivory. Loki's brilliant green eyes, the colour of ice-floes and the distant cold seas of his homelands, glittered with frustration and fury. Scars from the venom burns received during his long imprisonment bubbled down his left cheekbone, he rubbed them reflexively with his long, pale hand. He wore the beautifully embroidered, hand-woven ochre and red tunic and loose leggings of a Nordic prince, and a heavy gold and amber torc twisted round his straining neck. Gold and amber also gleamed from his fingers and wrists - a Viking king's ransom stolen from tarns and barrows long vanished in the great tides of time.

Then with a deafening sound like a thundercloud ripping and a rather theatrical puff of smoke, he blinked out of existence on this particular plane via, no doubt, the Cumbrian Stone gate. The room seemed to shiver and all the Nordic fitments and fittings returned to their real selves - prosaic Formica desk and table, plastic bucket chairs, polyester curtains. Only the great windows remained, and the view. A faint scent of ozone tickled the air.

Hester and Lydia burst into spontaneous applause.

Andvari sneezed.

'Excuse me, ladies. Allergic. I'll fetch the child now - if you don't mind waiting here.'

'Not at all' said Lydia. 'And - thank you, Andvari.'

The big man blushed. 'Oh, it's nothing.' He gazed at Lydia with his beautiful brown eyes. 'Anything for you, milady - I always thought the world of *you*...'

And with that he left, while Hester gave Lydia one of her old-fashioned looks. 'He's in love with you, isn't he?' she demanded.

Lydia cast her eyes down modestly and sighed. 'They all are, dear. It's the job description.'

Hester's reply was quite unsuitable for a respectable Widow and retired goddess.

Chapter Twelve

Hester and Lydia sat outside on the old swing seat with the big terracotta chiminea going full blast, fed with old apple branches from a fallen tree Hester had spotted on the waste land by the disused railway line on one of her walks and 'scavenged', as she put it daintily. Upstairs, in Lydia's spare room, an exhausted Joey Delaney slept dreamlessly, soothed by one of Hester's excellent nostrums and a small but effective Calming Glamour. Dion dozed with one eye open at the foot of the boy's bed - Joey had begged the friends piteously to 'let' the creature stay with him - as if anyone could make Dion do anything he didn't want to. Dion had sat, leaning against Joey's trembling legs as the boy perched on Lydia's sofa, sipping a mug of hot vegetable soup and blurting out his story in fits and starts, interspersed with tears of exhaustion and nervous reaction. The big cat's presence seemed to reassure Joey and he rubbed Dion's huge ears as he spoke, an attention Dion suffered amicably.

'It were Tiff an' Rav what started it after she got in with that lot at the Centre. She didn't like me seeing them, she said they were dirty heathens - but they're not, they're my mates. Tiff used to throw sweets up to me - she tried to throw a bottle of water but it didn't work and mum heard it when it fell so she locked the window after that, but I held up notes to Tiff asking her to go get you ladies, like - but mum saw one and then she took everything out of my room. She doesn't mean harm, she doesn't - she's not herself, honest, she - she - it's that fella, that Ray guy, he's - oh Miss Hester, he's a wrong 'un, honest, proper wicked. He says I'm full of devils, but I'm not, I'm not, am I? Mum believes him but she can't help it, can she?'

Joey's pitiful defence of the mother who had so willingly sold him to a complete stranger in return for the promise of youth and beauty touched the friends deeply. They knew no good would come of criticising Mrs. Delaney to her son, so wisely kept silent on the matter. Lydia's brief interview with the lady in question had not been so pleasant, and her recounting of the incident had brought Hester to the point of actual rage. Her face had been as white as the knuckles of the hand clutching her shawl.

Andvari had brought the struggling, half-fainting Joey to Loki's former lair and with a bow to the friends made his goodbyes and left - via a door rather than the puff of smoke favoured by his erstwhile master. The boy was utterly exhausted and the friends thought it best to take him straight to Lydia's to recover. They knew they'd have to return him to his mother - but the thought was not a pleasant one. With no father, and no relatives to speak of, Joey's options were not good.

'Lyddie,' said Hester after they had discussed what to do at length, 'will you go to see - that woman - or shall I?'

Lydia patted Hester's hand. 'I will, my dear. It won't be pleasant but I think of the two of us, she might respond best to me. I don't mean that rudely, but...'

'I know' said Hester. 'To be perfectly frank I'm rather relieved. I'm not sure I could behave as befits a lady.'

She smiled ruefully and refilled the kettle.

After a strong, fortifying cup of Assam and a spare brandy snap, Lydia had girded her proverbial loins and gone down the Terrace to Mrs. Delaney's house. Seeing a light was on, she knocked on the peeling front door.

Mrs. Delaney answered on the third knock, flinging the door open angrily. Lydia almost flinched at the sight of her - the woman was a shell even of the drab she had become. Her blood-shot eyes bulged from their shadowed sockets and the stringy cords in her crêpey neck stood out like straining hawsers. A yellow hand like a claw, the nails thick and cracked, grasped at her baggy blue skirt.

Her hair was a dry, greying thatch popped white at the ends and screwed back with a rubber band into a rough pony-tail. Her lips were pale and flaking and she ran a swollen red tongue over them convulsively. She smelt sour and unwashed. Although Lydia despised her, a wave of pity went through at the sight of what the foolish woman had become.

'Oh, it's you. What do you want? More interferin' ?' sneered Mrs. Delaney furiously. 'I got no time for this, I'm well busy.' And she made to shut the door.

Lydia stopped her. Although she often seemed to be spun out of sugar-gold and peachy softness, underneath, the actuality of what Lydia was meant no human creature could brook her if she was determined. Not that Mrs. Delaney was in any way aware of who actually stood on her filthy doorstep.

'It's about Joey, Mrs. Delaney. May I come in?'

Mrs. Delaney struggled with the door for a moment while Lydia stood unmoved and immovable holding it open. The woman almost cried with irritation, but after a curse of quite startling originality, grudgingly gave in. She glowered at Lydia balefully - the very picture, Lydia thought, of the village witch of hysteric imagination.

Stringy arms folded across her bony bosom, Mrs. Delaney moved back as Lydia entered and stood in the midst of the wreck of her living room. It stank of mould and dust, the windows were nailed shut with big, bent six-inch nails hammered through the frames at all angles. Clothes and household goods were strewn everywhere. Bottles lay on their sides disgorging bleach, vodka and milk respectively. A box of soap powder had exploded over the hearth rug unnoticed. The ripped curtains hung off the broken curtain rail unheeded. Two large battered suitcases, stuffed to bursting point, stood by the doorway. It was the chaos of frustration, thought Lydia. Mrs. Delaney simply didn't care anymore about this place. In her heart, she had already moved on. It didn't bode well for Joey.

'What do you want then, eh? I got no time to be messin' around,

I'm off with the Fellowship to find our Lord, for He has gone beyond an' we will follow.' Mrs. Delaney nodded emphatically. Her eyes were blazing dully like gas flares under dirty water with the annoyance of being baulked in her purpose.

'I'm here about your son...' began Lydia.

'My son? My son? I ain't got no son!' screeched Mrs. Delaney, pacing up and down the destroyed room, glass crunching unheeded under her feet as she strode about like a demented scarecrow. 'That devil ain't nowt to do with me - I won't have it back with me. You can't make me give shelter to the damned - I won't! I won't! Don't try to get clever with me, you - you - I made a bargain, I wrote my name - I'm going to be beautiful, beautiful, like Cheryl Cole - better than her even. She's an unbelieving slut, but I'm one of the true believers, I am, I'm going to have it all, everything - you can't make me give it up for that little bastard - full of devils he is. Wicked, wicked - I'm off, me, and when we find our Lord, all will be well. Brother Derek promised us, he did and I signed so I know....'

Lydia stepped in front of the desperately pacing woman, keeping her voice low and level. 'Joey is at my house, Mrs. Delaney. You must take him back. You need to seek help, the people you dealt with are tricksters and liars. Let me call a doctor to see you, I know someone kind and good who....'

Mrs. Delaney screamed. It was a piercing, fluting sound ripped from the woman's very soul, full of discordant frequencies and quite terrifying. 'Witch! Witch! I know you, devil! You won't trick me that way! They said the likes of you would try to stop us, but we're off to the Sanctuary - He will return, He will, and I *will* be beautiful an' rich an' have my pick of whoever I want! I'll have diamonds an' clothes fit for a queen an' be a celeb an' go to fancy parties an' everyone will worship me like they do all them in the magazines! What's that little get to me? Nothin'! Nothin' but trouble an - I hate him, I hate him, *he ruined my life!* I were young and pretty an' men wanted me - yes they did! I couldn't keep 'em off me - then I had him an' my figure was ruined an' there was him, always him draggin' at me, drainin' me dry an' his dad always nagging me to behave and stay in the house like a slave. I was a slave to those two and I had no fun anymore, no parties, no nothin'. No - no - nooooooooo!'

Her voice rose into another scream and she pushed past Lydia towards the door. 'Listen!' she cried, cupping her ear with her hand. 'It's the Fellowship van! I'm off an' you can't stop me! Take the little bastard if you want him so much, you an' your lezzer mate, disgustin', unnatural things you are! Take him, I don't want him, never did!'

She pulled and writhed as Lydia, deadly calm, held onto her arm. 'Do you renounce all claim on the child Joey, woman?' she said in a voice that would have frozen fire.

'What? What?' Mrs. Delaney screeched, an expression of puzzlement on her destroyed features.

'Do you give up all claim on the boy, your son?' repeated Lydia in a level voice. 'Look, look well, woman, *this* could be yours....'

Lydia made a complex gesture with her free hand and the air filled with the scent of a summer morning, clean, ozonic, peaceful. The room shimmered and a vision of gentle homeliness overlaid the ruin - a tidy, pleasant room, scent of baking, the laughter of a child, a sense of love and calm. Mrs. Delaney gaped, her body relaxing in Lydia's grip.

'Yes, this can happen. I will help you, you can have...'

Mrs. Delaney blinked rapidly. Lydia could almost hear her lids clicking over her dry eyes. 'I - I - I suppose... I mean, I ......No! No! I want to be pretty! I want - I want - no! You'll not fool me with your conjurin' tricks! You witch! You're a devil, they told us about the likes of you! Take the kid, I don't - I don't - just take him, I want - take him, you *bitch*!'

Had Mrs. Delaney been in any fit state, she would have realised that Lydia's voice was not that of the harmless, eccentric hippie woman she thought Lydia to be, but one which was charged with the power of eons, and that the face of the woman holding her with such a steely grip was like a golden burnished mask, beautiful and terrible. These things would, had she been in a normal state, have completely terrified her. But now all she was terrified of was losing her chance at the Fountain Of Youth. That fear made her blind and deaf to anything other than her own appalling, consuming need.

The Fountain Of Youth, thought Lydia grimly. How many had fallen prey to that delusion? As dear Gyremandel said, it is a bitter fever that disfigures before it kills, and only the strongest draught of reality can cure it. But no draught would be strong enough for the likes of Mrs. Delaney, who embraced the disease with a savage passion.

'I 'nounce the little sod now an' forever!' cried Mrs. Delaney, and squirmed from Lydia's grasp, leaving her baggy grey cardigan in Lydia's hand. Seizing her suitcases she ran full tilt out of the door and scrambled into a large blue and orange minibus sign-written with the slogan, 'The Lokey Fellowship Foundation' and packed with people all dressed in numbing shades of sludge, their blister-white faces pressed anxiously against the steamy windows. It drove off with a squeal of tyres, swaying dangerously.

Lydia stood in the mess and stink and felt her heart sink. Of course, she could care for dear Joey and, if necessary, find him a good home - but she could not help feeling dreadfully sorry for Mrs. Delaney. The woman had been driven mad by the promise of the impossible as many another had before her - Lydia remembered many famous women who had been tricked the same way - Lucrezia, Erzsébet, Catherine - all had fallen prey to the same desire and done terrible things in the name of preserving their youthful beauty. Murderous things. Giving away your child was nothing in comparison to what Erzsébet had done, for example, the wicked soul. But Mrs. Delaney wasn't a great queen or an infamous countess. She was just a simple woman, not very clever or educated, driven mad by lies and false promises. Now her life would be ruined utterly.

Lydia sighed. She herself embodied all that the Mrs. Delaneys of the world desired - she could be as young and beautiful as she wished to be, in any culture she chose - she could be a Hollywood film star, a Zulu Princess, a Chinese Tai-Tai, a Maori Queen. Anything. She had indeed been many things and meant the world to many men, human and divine. Her immortality and her role as the goddess of love meant she could have easily what any human woman in the modern world would give everything for. Yet she lived alone. She looked like a nice, rather arty, middle-aged woman, still pretty, still attractive, but hardly a voluptuous man-eating diva. Dion was her old companion and her lover, but he was not what most women would consider, well, reliable. That made her smile again. *Dearest Dion, such a wild thing, always was. Maybe that's why I love him. I really can't ever have him fully, he's an outside cat, he comes and goes as he pleases,* she thought, and with that she took a deep breath and wove a complex and multi-dimensional glyph in the air. The scent of eucalyptus, sere and cleansing, filled the mould-smelling air and cleared it, then the gentle odour of lavender followed in a shimmering violet haze. The house seemed to shiver, then suddenly all was neat, clean and perfect, just as it had been in the vision she had offered to Mrs. Delaney. The living room sparkled and shone and the cruel, nailed windows were back to normal. Pretty rose-coloured curtains blew out slightly in the fresh grass-scented breeze and Lydia knew the whole house would now be a testament to excellent housekeeping - even if it had been achieved by rather unusual methods.

She stepped outside, to find the dusk falling in a soft blue veil over the little cul-de-sac. As she turned and shut the front door she felt a presence behind her - or rather two presences. Smiling to herself, she turned to find Rav and Tiff gazing at her anxiously, their little faces creased with worry.

'Miss Lydia, Miss, is Joey alright? We saw his mum go off in that van, we - is he alright, please?' Tiff's voice quavered with unshed tears and it was all she could do to preserve her tomboy dignity. Rav's round face was unashamedly unhappy and his soft cheeks were wet.

Lydia went to the old, rickety unpainted garden bench under the front window and sat down. Rav and Tiff sat either side of her, their dark eyes full of questions. Lydia put an arm round each of them and drew the children close.

'Well, Joey is at my house now, sleeping. I'm not going to pretend he hasn't had a very difficult time, but everything will be fine, my dears, and thanks to your help and courage, he always knew people cared for him and would help him. That's what got him through - your not forgetting him.'

Tiff sniffed miserably and tugged on the end of her long, shining plait. 'But Miss Lydia Miss, his mum...' Rav nodded in agreement.

Lydia smiled sadly. 'Mrs. Delaney has gone away, I'm afraid. I don't know when she'll come back, so for the meantime, Miss Hester and I will look after Joey. You can come and see him anytime. Such brave people as yourselves are always welcome in our home. He'll be so happy to see you - really, he talked of nothing else but how clever and strong you both were.'

Tiff thought a moment while Rav studied her solemnly, wondering what his queen would say next. It was often hard being her lieutenant, but he believed in her utterly. She was magnificent. He thought she was like a tiger in a girl's skin - inscrutable, fierce and strong. He sighed. What a woman.

'Miss - did you get Joey's box out of the house for him?' she said, thoughtfully.

'His box? Oh, yes, his Memory Box! Yes, he told me about it once - it's full of string if I recall correctly. No. Why, dear, should I?'

Tiff stood up and pulled at Lydia's sleeve excitedly. 'Oh, Miss - Miss - he'll want it, more than anything - it's not just string, honest, it's got all his stuff in it, letters from his dad, his best comics, a football programme from Man United, his old Action Man - oh everything! And I know where it is, he hid it from his mum when she started going funny, he told me where it was before she - before she stopped him seeing us - can we go and get it for him, please, please?'

Rav was nodding so hard Lydia was slightly fearful his head might drop off. 'Yes, Miss, honest Miss, he proper loves that stuff, Miss, he does. It's under the loose floorboard under his bed it is' he said stoutly.

Tiff reached round and kicked Rav's shin as hard as she could. He groaned in a long-suffering way and clutched his leg.

'Tiffany - please. Don't be so unkind!' admonished Lydia, trying not to laugh, given poor Rav's pain.

Tuff pouted. 'Well, honest, he's hopeless. He'd tell anyone, he'd tell the postman - we were supposed to keep it secret.'

Rav moaned. 'But it's Miss Lydia, Tiff, it's not anyone. Sorry. But it's…'

Tiff forgave him, as she always did, moved to pity by his sweet round face and unfailing devotion. 'Oh - Rav, honestly... but Miss Lydia, will you get the box? Please, Joey'll fret for it otherwise. He's very sensitive, he is. Very.' she said reverently.

Lydia looked at the shining faces gazing at her so hopefully. A small pain, one she was very used to, but which still managed to nip at her heart, ran through her. Children - but it was not to be, not for her. The love she represented was not the milky tenderness of mother-love, it was the golden, ephemeral but powerful prelude - but that did not stop her feeling, sometimes, a great and poignant sadness for something she had not been made to fulfil. It was a kind of ghost-loss, a phantom void in her soul.

She smiled and tugged Tiff's plait. 'OK, back in a minute.' And she quickly went back into the house and up to Joey's now sparklingly clean bedroom where the odour of socks and boy had been replaced by a faint essence of fresh cotton and lavender. It took moments to locate and retrieve the box from what Joey obviously fondly thought was the incredibly secret hiding place under the squeaky floorboard: only a child would imagine it would conceal anything from an adult set on finding out what was being concealed, and that innocence cut Lydia to the heart. She really must do her best by the boy - if she and Hester did not, who would?

Locking the front door behind her Lydia was confronted by the sight of Rav and Tiff, torn between the calls of their mothers summoning them for tea and the worry that Miss Lydia, being a grown up and therefore not terribly bright about some things, might not have found the box.

'Miss, Miss - we've got to go, it's dinner - you got it - ace - can we come see him tomorrow, please? Please?' Tiff begged, hopping from foot to foot desperately.

'Of course you ....' Lydia smiled as the Dynamic Duo dashed off to their homes without letting her finish her sentence.

She looked at the box intently. Was she mistaken, or did the faintest of faint vibrations linger in the battered old wood? Did she sense a hint, less than that even, of a Glamour that hummed distantly like the sound of the sea heard from over a hill? Was that a whiff, bleached out and attenuated, of roses - old, almost purple, red roses? And why was it so annoyingly and unplaceably familiar?

She turned and walked quickly down the Terrace to home and Hester.

Chapter Thirteen

'The question is, should we open it?' asked Lydia, rather anxiously. 'As I see it, it's the boy's private property, yet…'

Hester got up, fed another branch into the fire and then reseated herself thoughtfully. Wrapping her old black shawl around herself more tightly, she sniffed and then tutted. Lydia knew that meant she was thinking hard.

'I rather feel - that is, under the exceptional circumstances - that we might be permitted to open it,' Hester sighed. 'Yes, Joey's well-being is our primary concern and though of course a person's privacy is paramount - no, I think we should.'

The friends studied the battered wooden box carefully. Both now agreed there was indeed a lingering Glamour on it, but so faint as to be almost undetectable. The box itself was remarkable in that it was obviously very, very old: not very big, easy to carry or hide, it was made of a much battered and discoloured dark oak wood, bound with hammered iron bands and closed with an iron hasp, obviously of antique manufacture. Perhaps the Glamour was a residue of former owners and nothing to do with Joey at all? That must be the case, they decided. The lad must have come by the box innocently enough at some junk shop or jumble sale - strange things like that did happen, why only the other day in the newspaper, they had read of a woman who had bought a Fabergé gold and diamond brooch for fifty pence at a Church rummage sale. Perhaps this box was a valuable antique? Only an expert from the Antiques Road-show could tell the friends - themselves valuable antiques in many ways - that.

They opened the box. Tiff had been right, it wasn't entirely full of string, though there was a great deal of assorted twine. There was also a broken pocket knife, a lump of putty, an old red bandanna, some marbles (various, including a rather nice blue Bovey Lace), a football match programme, a note from Tiff (which they carefully refolded and put back immediately) and some birthday and Christmas cards, which they took out and examined.

The cards were all written in the same hand - a bold cursive, black ink, all the envelopes postmarked Drogheda, Ireland. They seemed to start when Joey was around three and stop around two years ago. They were all signed '*Your loving Da, Angus*'. The one with the most recent postmark asked why Joey was not answering - did he not get the parcel with the bow and arrows Angus' mate had made specially for him? There was a phone number on the facing page to the message and a note under it, '*Ring me, son, anytime. If I'm not there your nana will take a message. She loves you too, don't forget.*'

The friends looked at each other.

'Well, shall I do it, or will you?' asked Hester pointedly.

Lydia looked at the card in her had. It was a vivid green with a design of cheerful foil-printed shamrocks and the caption 'Top O'The Mornin' To You, Birthday Boy!' She turned it over and over in her hands.

'Hester, there's something here - something I can't quite grasp - do you feel it?'

Hester's face in the dusk and the flickering firelight was thoughtful. 'Yes, I do - but it doesn't feel negative, in fact if anything, it feels strangely familiar, in a way I can't explain. But none the less, feelings or no, it is our duty to re-unite Joey with his blood family. The father obviously cares for him and I would strongly suspect that Mrs. Delaney simply cut off all contact with him and probably threw any parcels and further cards away to avoid having to deal with Joey's questions. Then when his father died... But the grandmother may still be living, and who knows how many other relatives. We must ring that number, Lydia. We cannot keep the boy and you know it.'

A tear tracked silently down Lydia's cheek; she knew Hester was right, and she knew what an effort it cost Hester to say it - she, too, would happily have taken Joey in forever. But in the modern world, women couldn't go around randomly rescuing children and bringing them up willy-nilly; there were agencies, and forms, and legal safeguards, and - Lydia took her mobile phone from her jeans pocket, and dialled.

'Ah, hello, yes - I'm trying to find the grandmother of Joseph Delaney - yes, England - I - oh, of course (*it's a young woman, they've gone to get the grandmother, I...*), Yes, Mrs. Delaney? Oh, Mrs. Maccan, I'm sorry, my name is Lydia Larkin, I'm - oh, please, don't worry, Joey is fine, yes, but - yes - we're trying to find his relatives as - no, I'm simply a neighbour, a friend of Joey - no, his mother has, well, she has abandoned him and - yes, I agree, but - since his father has passed away, you must be - I'm sorry? No, we were told - oh, oh, I see, yes, she did in fact tell Joey - yes, wicked - is it possible to speak with your son? Oh, of course, I'll hold.'

Lydia held her phone away from her ear and hissed at Hester. 'The father, he's not dead at all, that dreadful woman lied. They're going to get him, he's in his shed or something.'

Hester's face spoke volumes, but she said nothing. Pallas Athene shone in her eyes like burnished silver; had the absent Mrs. Delaney been present she would have learned a most painful lesson about truth and falsehood.

Lydia gestured excitedly, the phone back at her ear. 'Mr. Delaney? Oh, Mr. Maccan, I - you *are* Joey Delaney's father? Her name, not yours - oh, I see. I'm so sorry, but your - your ex-partner told Joey you had been killed in a car crash and - Angus, of course - I - Angus - wait, I know your voice, I know - forgive me asking but are you sometimes called Aengus Mac Og, by any chance? Oh, right, well, yes. Angus, it's Lydia, yes, you know, and I have Athene here with me and my lord Dion and your son. Can you come now? I suggest the Cumbrian Stone gate, it seems to be in working order.

Yes, I'll be expecting you.'

Lydia folded up the little pink clam-shell phone and looked at Hester, who stared at her with a mixture of exasperation and despair. Lydia shrugged, spreading her shapely hands in a helpless gesture.

'No wonder there was a Glamour on that box: Joey is in fact the son of Aengus Mac Og, Irish god of love and general all round loveable rogue. More girlfriends than there are leaves on that tree and one of the handsomest creatures I have ever set eyes on. Full of charm and blather. Well, no wonder Joey inspires such love and loyalty, really, in some ways I'm not at all surprised. In others I'm - what does Mrs. Baggot say? I'm proper gob smacked. Really. Angus. Who would have thought… He's just got to sort out something and then he's on his way.'

'I shall put the kettle on then,' said Hester, stoutly, radiating an air of disapproval - love gods and goddesses, indeed! It appeared the place was heaving with them. Just then Dion sidled round the acanthus and Hester harrumphed; *and another*, she thought. Just what we need. Where's dear Gyremandel's Rule Of Logic now, eh? Oh, it'll be a nest of charm and behaviour in seconds as soon as that damned Irishman gets here - and what about Joey? How will he take having his father back? Does no-one but myself have any sense?

'You'd best break out the brandy, Hester dear. I'm sure Angus would like a nip after his travels' Lydia carolled at Hester's back.

Then, with a silent rush of air and a sharp smell of ozone, Aengus Mac Og, Irish love god, appeared by the birch tree, dressed in blue jeans, an old white Aran sweater and worn tan work boots. His curling black hair shone in the solar lights and his impossibly adorable brown face, replete with high cheekbones, chiselled chin and black-lashed twinkling blue eyes, smiled at Lydia with a warmth that had her toes curling in her Ugg boots. He smelt of salt sea air, the outdoors and, faintly, of peat fires. Dion growled softly at her side. Not just Hester was unimpressed by provincial love gods, it seemed.

'Ah, my queen, as beautiful as ever - no, *more* beautiful, to my mind - and to think it was yourself that saved my boy - can I ever thank you enough?' Aengus' voice was like thick honey falling off a warm spoon and his brogue added a charm all its own.

Hester, returning with a tray of tea and the brandy bottle, was exasperated to see Lydia positively simper and extend her hand to be kissed, which it was, lingeringly. Rather too lingeringly. With a shower of sparks, Dion materialised in his human form, looking cross.

Aengus swiftly let go of Lydia's hand. 'Ah, my lord Dionysius, a great pleasure! It's been - well, a very long time. And here's Athene! Quite the Olympian gathering, eh? Well, thank you, my lady, a nip would be most welcome…But really, I cannot thank you enough, I really cannot - the boy is close to my heart - I have few sons, and lately, well… Joseph is the last in a long time, good boy that he is. I love him dearly.'

Seated now, the gods and goddesses looked to any watching eyes like friends chatting round the garden fire. If you ignored the fact that Dion, seated cross-legged on the floor, was stark naked except for his vine wreath, and that the dusk light around the unearthly group had a curious violet tinge. The scent of hyacinths and oud filled the air and faint twinkling sparks still fluttered round Dion's shaggy head.

Hester leant towards Aengus interrogatively. 'Forgive me for saying so, but how did you come to choose Mrs. Delaney as a consort? Surely….'

Aengus laughed and birds swooned in the trees. Hester ignored them. 'Ah well, now - direct as ever my lady! But 'tis a good question indeed. It was more like, she found me. Oh, she was a good-lookin' girl when I spied her at the dance - I was over here on a little business, and a man has to relax, so I went to a dancehall to look at the fillies, I'll be honest with you there, and she fairly flung herself at me - and I ask you, being as I am, how could I say no? But I found out quick enough that the hair, the face, the bosom and the charms all came off at night, as they say. Under the camouflage she was a hard little thing and she got with child on our first night, no boasting intended.'

Aengus winked, and took a sip of brandy. Lydia giggled. Dion said absolutely nothing. In the grass by his hard, dusty feet, small insects ran for their lives.

'So I knew almost straightway, and I knew it was a boy, so I stuck by her, thinking I could bring her out of her shell as it were, educate her a bit, maybe - who knows - settle down for a while. I've done it before, it has its attractions, even to such as me. But she was as thick as a branch of that tree, just lived for the dancing and flirting, drank like a fish and didn't understand who I was at all, or want anything from me but money and gifts. A cold-hearted piece. After my boy was born - and a fine little man he was - she was straight back to her old ways. I told her I'd not stand it and she laughed, asked me if I thought I was Brad Pitt or someone, not just a Mick on the make in England as she put it. Brad Pitt! Well, we all know who *he* is, don't we? So I took myself off home to see to my interests there - I have a stud farm, lovely ponies - and next thing I know, it's don't you come back, I have another fella now and you're not wanted. Broke my heart. Not for her, you understand, but for my boy. I wrote cards and sent presents, thinking to come and get him but she rang my ma and told her in no uncertain terms, I was forbidden to see him. I was planning to come get him anyway - but then you called, my queen.'

Hester snorted. 'You took your time about it. She treated the boy abominably and now she's run off with one of Loki's cults - an energy-stealing cult, I'm sure you know what I mean. You must take responsibility for your son. He cannot stay here, you must take him with you.'

Hester spoke harshly but Lydia - and Dion - could see how much it cost her to part with the child. Her face was adamantine but her white fingers plucked fiercely at the worn tassles of her shawl.

Aengus raised a perfectly arched eyebrow. 'Loki, is it? That auld rascal? I mind having dealings with him some centuries back in Ireland, in Dublin it was, up to the same tricks, posing as a quack doctor selling potions to the gullible. Well, no doubt he's promised the silly mare eternal youth or some such - ah, he did, I'm not surprised. But my lady Athene, you misjudge me, I do want my boy. He's the apple of my eye, the joy of my heart. His nana can't wait to see him, and his sisters too. I have a nice room for him all done and a pretty little horse of his own. He'll have a great life, so he will. And you'll come and visit him? It would be an honour for us to have such distinguished Olympians in our home.'

Hester rolled her eyes. In the great ash tree, the owl hooted. Stars twinkled overhead in curious configurations that caused an amateur astronomer in the neighbourhood to consult her books anxiously.

Aengus took a sip of his brandy and gazed winningly at Hester who ignored his charm, which she could feel stealing round her warm and sensual as a cat purring on her knee - and about as meaningful. Minor gods like Aengus could not help but be what they were - and the world was full of them. Some, like Aengus and the god now calling himself Brad Pitt, knew perfectly well who and what they were, and continued - pretty much - to live the lives they always had. Some had chosen to give up the memory of themselves when their worshippers had deserted them for other faiths, as indeed, she had, and instead became simply playboys and womanisers, crediting their romantic successes to their good looks or powers of seduction. In their human form they got physically older, though at a much slower rate than a genuine human, and they eventually died, or rather the human shell did. But their divine essence was endlessly re-born, since immortality cannot be revoked, merely changed. It wasn't an easy path. There were the endless re-births down the ages and the struggle with, or against, the buried memories…. Hester was very glad she had reclaimed herself. She would never go back to that existence again, never. It had seemed like the right thing to do at the time, and she had been very angry that her devotees had denied the path of logic and fled to the emotional chaos of the new, fashionable god, but it would have been better to stick it out, like Lydia had. Aengus too, for that matter. He himself was winking at her - she summoned a withering glare. It had no effect at all.

'A penny for your thoughts, my lady,' Aengus said cheerfully.

Hester harrumphed. 'Indeed. Now, what will we tell the authorities about Joey, when they ask? A missing child is a very serious matter indeed - there will be questions, various social care agencies - his school.'

Dion spoke in English. It was so unusual that everyone - even Aengus - stared at him amazed. Naturally, as a god, Dion had the facility of language, but in all the time Lydia had been with him he had only spoken in a language other than Olympian Greek once, and that was to swear briefly in High German during the late 1300's. His voice had a curious, golden quality, clear and ringing, like a cymbal being struck with a crystal rod. It was intensely masculine, without being at all macho. It was quiet, but every nuance was clear and brilliant in the listener's minds. It was as if he spoke simultaneously on two planes, the physical and mental.

'They will not care' he said quietly. 'They will not seek him. He is as nothing to them, a boy-child of the peasant classes. If no-one speaks of him, and they will not, it will be as if he never existed. Euoi, it is as nothing, he is a mote in dust of time. I have put a binding on the minds of all here who knew my queen's fosterling: his pedagogues, his physicians, even the children who were his friends. They now believe he has moved away to a better life with distant relatives in a faraway land. They are happy for him.'

Dion's face was an archaic bronze mask in the firelight and he radiated the kind of power that springs from the natural world, that of great predators, or volcanoes and typhoons; ancient, made of the bones of the earth. Lydia remembered he was even older than she was, one of the first gods, the very essence of nature in all its chaos and unimaginable energies. Hester, humbled, bowed her head to the boy whose earthly shape contained such unimaginable forces.

Aengus cleared his throat nervously. 'My lord Dionysus, you do my people great honour concerning yourself with such matters - I - I - thank you. My son thanks you, as does all my Clan. We are in your debt.'

Dion rose and stood, his eyes like blue silk shot with gold, his face unreadable. He was so strange and otherworldly, there was no point of contact the others could find. What were the doings of the noisy modern world to him, who had roamed the slopes of the great mountains in sun and snow, creating storms and flowers alike simply for his own amusement when humans were just grunting animals hiding in caves, afraid of fire and the star-stitched night?

'There is no debt. I did it because my queen loves the human child. What she loves, I protect. The boy is your son, Maccan. His welfare is now yours.'

And with that he vanished, silently and without any disturbance of the aether, the velvet night enfolding him utterly.

There was a silence as the others strove to understand the huge Glamour Dion had created without a second thought - something Lydia and Hester would have had to prepare for weeks and would have worried themselves to bits over. Dion's Glamour had simply radiated out along myriad connections associated with Joey, through time and space, backwards and forwards, up and down, like a four dimensional cat's cradle, affecting dozens of humans and deftly re-weaving the very fabric of the Universe. Just because Lydia loved the child. And how Lydia loved Dion. Tears welled up in her beautiful eyes and flowed unchecked at the thought of his centuries of devotion to her. Hester silently handed her another of Mr. Marvell's large, snowy handkerchiefs.

'Don't get mascara on it,' Hester said in a voice that might, had you known her well, have seemed a trifle unsteady.

'I'm not wearing any,' snuffled Lydia behind swathes of immaculate cotton. 'Just as well. Oh, Hester! Dion - it's astonishing. I didn't think he'd concern himself…'

'He loves you, my lady, as we all do,' said Aengus, his own eyes suspiciously damp. 'He says there's no debt, but I shall never forget and none of my people will either.'

'More tea?' said Hester, and poured Lydia a cup which also contained a drop of Marvell's Calming & Soothing Nostrum, a small blue glass bottle of which was always in her capacious pocket.

'Thank you, dear.' Lydia sipped the first flush Darjeeling gratefully. 'Aengus - will you take Joey now? If you just…'

Aengus smiled. 'Yes, I know, ladies. I will see to it he understands what he should in a quiet way, just like I would with a young horse, gentle and steady. He will be fine, sure he will. He's my blood after all, he will have had an inkling of it. Did he not have his own little clan and a young lady half in love with him already? He's my boy, alright.'

'More than half in love,' Lydia smiled too, rather ruefully. 'Oh, poor Tiff - but she will be consoled by his memory and the thought that he's having a wonderful life in - well, wherever. And the memory will fade in time - humans can't hold onto these things in their minds for long, especially at her age. And Rav too - he really hero-worshipped Joey. But now at least he'll have Tiff all to himself.'

'Aengus Mac Og, you must take the boy now. Here is his box of memories, he is upstairs - see the lighted window there - that's where he's sleeping. Don't wake him just - just…' Hester's resolve faltered.

Aengus put his shapely brown hands on her shoulders and she felt a warmth of love steal through her, comforting and gentle. Love, she thought, sighing, comes in many guises. She didn't fight it and accepted his kiss on her cheek. Then he bowed and kissed Lydia's hand again and went into the house and up the stairs.

The friends sat together on the swing seat facing the back of the little terraced house as they had so many nights before. Lydia held Hester's hand and Hester let her. They watched the window behind which Joey, their dearly beloved foster son, lay sleeping, unaware of his wonderful new life to come. The window suddenly glowed golden, and a whiff of ozone filled the air. Sparks glittered behind the glass, then the light returned to normal.

Joey was gone.

Chapter Fourteen

Autumn came in splendour that year, the trees dressed in exquisitely modish outfits of ochre, crimson and gold that caused comment and made Mr. Baggott remark that he was fairly set to believe in that global warming stuff as, to his mind, such hues weren't natural. In The Lakes, happen, but not in town. The smell of bonfires laced the cool, still air with a woody incense and Hester busied herself filling orders for Marvell's Nourishing Beauty Crème and Marvell's Rose & Lavender Cooling Lotion. Lydia painted a number of canvasses depicting imaginary landscapes, very magical looking and pretty, and sold them all to a wealthy young couple who wanted Art for their new home in Umbria. Hester thought the sum they paid excessive but Lydia gave it all to a children's charity she patronised and so Hester made her a voluminous new painting apron as a reward.

They didn't talk about Joey.

Rav and Tiff came to tell them the amazing news that Joey had 'hemigrated' to New Zealand to live with an aunt and uncle he didn't even know he had but it was brilliant, and proper Lord Of The Rings. The Delaney house was sold - presumably by Mrs. Delaney to fund her activities - and a young Polish couple with a newborn baby moved in, exclaiming over how beautifully clean and well-decorated it was. It smelt so nice of lavender, the pretty young mother said in her charming accent to Hester when she took a welcome basket of muffins, the previous owner must have been very house-proud. Hester hmm'd non-committally and welcomed the new family to the Terrace. She told Lydia the baby looked just like Winston Churchill and they agreed that new babies often did, but it would doubtless improve in time.

Slowly the nights drew in and it was no longer feasible to sit outside round the chiminea. Dion took on his winter fur, thick and soft as night itself, and the friends had their tea and cakes in Lydia's little front room, Lydia lounging on the deep-cushioned red sofa, Hester on a ladder-back chair she brought in from the kitchen. Tonight they were nibbling chestnut torte fresh from the oven and drinking a malty, fortifying Assam. A wood fire burnt in the grate and the room smelt delightfully of sandalwood and sagebrush. Dion dozed - apparently - on the big sheepskin rug by the hearth.

After a silence while they ate thoughtfully, Lydia spoke. Hester had been waiting for her to say something, and she knew what Lyddie was about to discuss with her. She wrapped her old shawl about her thin figure more tightly and smoothed her Domestic Goddess apron over her bony knees.

'My dear,' began Lydia, 'you know why I bought this house. There is a very powerful and unused Portal located just under where we are seated. I have done some research and it is, in fact, the lost Kingsfoil Portal, which as you know, was last documented by our dear Gyremandel in his Meditations And Prophecies.'

Hester frowned. 'He said it was legend, not fact, if you recall.'

'Indeed he did. He could not state the reality for fear of being thought a heretic and a warlock, which as you know also, was his eventual fate anyway, the poor dear man. No, it's the Kingsfoil alright. And I have the key.'

'Ah' said Hester.

'Indeed' replied Lydia, taking a sip of tea. 'Hester - my lord Dion - we could go anytime. Now, if we wished. We could join the others in the place beyond, never to return. Ever. I know we - well, my lord and I certainly - chose to remain on earth with the humans in the hopes of seeing the project through and - in my case - perhaps helping and guiding them a little. You, Hester, chose the third path of forgetfulness. Well, I didn't manage to do much useful helping and guiding to be honest, and I wonder, is it time to leave now?

What good is it hanging around watching them be born and live and die, generation after generation? Have they forged world peace? Or an end to starvation? No. At least in Elysion, we could be - we could - well, it's very relaxing, apparently. No stress. Nothing but niceness, and everyone we used to know having a pleasant time. Rather like an expensive Spa. But we couldn't come back. Once you go over, that's it, it's a one-way ticket.'

There was a silence as everyone gazed at the fire flickering in the grate.

'Well, it sounds most restful, I must say,' said Hester. 'Can one do anything one likes?'

'I believe so,' said Lydia thoughtfully. 'But of course the laws of time and space that exist here don't exist there, so most people don't do a lot, rather they dream a great deal or commune with, er, the greater universe and suchlike.'

'No books, then?' Hester enquired.

'Um, not to my knowledge. I don't think they're needed, as it were. I mean, you *wouldn't* need them, would you? Or anything like that, I suppose. Not that I'm an expert but I do remember what Zeus said about it, and Hera was especially keen to get a good rest as I recall. I mean - it does sound - well, I don't know, very relaxing.'

'How hard would it be to summon up the Portal?' asked Hester. 'Purely as a kind of preview, of course. Just so we could see.'

'Not hard at all, since I have the key. I could do it now. Shall I?'

'Oh, do. Thank you. Dion, my lord, are you agreeable?' said Hester, with the new-found respect for Dion she had since the night Joey left them. Dion nodded, his eyes slits of fire.

Lydia spoke the key and made the appropriate glyph. The air filled with an intense aroma of salt and figs, and the wall to the garden shimmered in colours never seen by the human eye and seemed to stretch outwards into infinity. It was rather disconcerting, in an end-terrace house in a small town in England in winter. Dion loped across to Lydia, and Hester joined them on the sofa, all of them staring at the silently spinning place that offered them a way to eternal bliss.

The Portal coiled and twisted in and out of infinity like a Moebius strip gone mad. Hester could see - or thought she could see - rolling hills and mellow fields in the far distance of the Portal's eye. Lydia thought she could hear the fatherly tones of Lord Zeus, but she couldn't make out what he was saying. They all felt the atmosphere, long forgotten, of their home on Olympus - not exactly *on* Olympus of course - the scent of wild hyacinth, the pure ancient uncorrupted, unpolluted mountain air, the warmth of the sun, the taste of Chian wine and nectar, the chanting of the faithful. It was a bittersweet sensation, for they had loved that time, but it could never return and so it was go on as they were - or step through to Elision, forever.

The Portal turned at greater and greater speed, all the more powerful for its utter silence. Hester felt herself drawn towards the promise of eternal peace and quiet. No more humans, no more television, no more cars and noise, no more Mrs. Delaneys, no more heartbreak or oven burns or bills to pay. Just peace, dozing Time away in golden sunsets. It was - it was....

'I can't' said Lydia. 'I'm sorry. I just can't. Not yet. I - it's - I'm sorry but it sounds so *dull*. Like a cruise or something. Oh, I know I'm being childish, I know - and I will have to go one day but - I can't, not yet. I really want to see what happens to the humans, I still think they might yet pull through. I'd just worry about them if I went now - I'm sorry, my friends, but I can't. I don't want to, I just don't. You can - of course you can - but no. I won't.'

Hester came to with a start. 'Lydia - are you sure? Think of what a rest it would be, and...' Hester's eyes were drawn, irresistably, back to the whirling brilliance of the Portal. There it was, she had only to step through....

'Oh, you go, really - don't let me influence you - I mean, we'd see each other again eventually of course. But really, I just - oh - I just can't. Not yet.'

Hester looked again at the Portal. She sighed. She knew what she was going to do. 'I'm not going either. Well, not yet as you say. We can do some good, we can help the humans. I know we can. In small ways. We helped Joey, didn't we? And Mrs. Baggott? There might be others - what if we left and they needed us? You're right, Lyddie, we can go another time.' She drew herself up, her shawl wrapped as tight as armour around her thin frame, her grey eyes valiant. 'Yes. Definitely. Another time.'

Lydia rested her hand on the great cat's head. 'And you, my lord?'

The answer came in her mind and Hester's as she knew it would. 'Whither you go, my queen, go I. I am not yet apt for Elysion. We will tarry here awhile yet.' And he yawned prodigiously, showing huge white fangs and a lot of clean, pink tongue. Lydia had the strong suspicion then, that Dion didn't need the Portal - if he wanted to go, he just would. She said the words and made the sign. As if it had never been, the Portal winked out of existence on the mortal plane. An odour of warm honey and the faint murmuring of bees fading into unutterable distances was all that remained.

Hester and Lydia looked at one another.

'I shall put the kettle on, then' said Hester.

And she did.

Euoi.

Miss Larkin's
Raspberry and Chocolate Gateau

175g butter
175g dark chocolate, chopped
3 eggs
half teaspoon of proper vanilla extract
350g caster sugar
125g plain flour
40g self-raising flour
100g ground amonds
125g raspberries (plus extra for serving)

Preheat oven to 180C/350F/gas mark 4,
and line a 20cm/8" round cake tin with non-stick baking paper.
Melt butter and chocolate in a Bain Marie,
or in a bowl over a saucepan of boiling water.
Stir till melted, then leave to cool.
Put eggs, vanilla extract, and sugar in a bowl.
Beat until mixture is light and thick, then fold through the flour,
ground almonds, chocolate mixture, and half of the raspberries.
Pour mixture into the cake tin, sprinkling the remaining
raspberries over the top, and bake for 35 minutes,
or until the top of the cake is firm to the touch.

Allow to cool before cutting, then serve with lots of thick cream.

Remember to save some for Dion.

The Widow Marvell's
All-Purpose Salve

10g cocoa butter
30g unrefined beeswax
10ml jojoba oil
10ml almond oil
10ml peach kernel oil
5ml sweet almond oil

Melt the unrefined beeswax in a Bain Marie.
Add cocoa butter to this and stir until it combines,
then heat again for a minute.
Remove from the heat, add all the other ingredients,
one at a time, and stir well.
Pour the mixture into a sterilised jar and let it cool.

If you wish, add a drop or two of your favourite essential oil
during the final stirring. I prefer Rose Absolute,
but Lavender is also delightful.

Miss Larkin's
Yoghurt Cake With Lemon Syrup Drizzle

for the cake:
225g plain non-fat yoghurt
250g sugar
3 eggs, beaten
35g melted butter or margarine
450g all-purpose flour, sifted
1 teaspoon baking soda

for the lemon syrup:
150g sugar
300ml water
3 tablespoons strained lemon juice

Preheat oven to 375F.
Beat the yoghurt and sugar in a large bowl, then add eggs, butter,
flour, and baking soda, beating well after each addition.
Pour resulting batter into a greased cake tin,
and bake for 30 minutes or until the cake is golden on top.
Let it cool in the tin,
and boil the syrup ingredients together for five minutes.
Remove from heat, and drizzle hot syrup over cooled cake.
Cover and chill for at least two hours.

Cut into diamond shapes,
decorate with edible gold sprinkles and serve.

The Widow Marvell's
Wholly Unnecessary Body Glitter
(by request of Miss Lydia Larkin)

3 tablespoons of aloe vera gel
half a teaspoon of very fine glitter, colour as desired
one drop of essential oil (optional)
food colouring (optional)

Stir to blend, then store at room temperature
in a small, airtight jar or container.

Do not use near the eyes or any sensitive personal area.